BORN OF
BLOOD

THE LEAGUE
NEMESIS RISING

SHERRILYN
KENYON

OLIVERHEBERBOOKS

Prologue

There were days when it didn't pay to be human.
Or Andarion.

And definitely not any combination of the two.

Today was just that day for Jayne Erixour. And as fire, blood, and unidentifiable body parts rained down upon her, she wished herself anywhere but where she was.

Closing her eyes, she tried her best to imagine another life. Another world.

Some safe place where children were wanted and protected. Where people were cherished, and they had someone they could put

their faith in.

Where betrayal was unknown and kindness was a given, not the exception. A place where life was something someone valued and not a cheap commodity that was bought and sold without a second thought.

Or worse, something thrown aside with reckless disregard.

Where every life didn't have a price.

"Jayne!"

1

She opened her eyes at the sound of a warning call that preceded an incoming bomb screeching overhead. Her heart pounding, she dove for cover an instant before it impacted a few yards away.

Screams filled her ears as the dampeners she'd embedded in her eustachian tubes shielded her eardrums from the percussive damage. She choked on the sudden tears that came with the aftermath, refusing to let them fall. This was war and she was a soldier.

Even if she was only fourteen.

At least that was the lie she told herself. But inside, she was still a girl wanting to be home again. Safe. Protected. Wanting to feel her father's arms around her.

Wanting to hear her mother telling her that everything was good, and that life was worth living. That the morning would come and return light to the landscape.

But that wasn't today.

Today it sucked so much that she couldn't even find a reason why she was fighting so hard for one more stinking breath.

Why bother?

A sane person would walk out and let the bombs end it all. One shot and all the pain and misery would be over.

Just one step.

One shot.

"I'm too young for this shit." And she was tired beyond belief.

"Damn it, Jaynie!"

She barely heard those words before she felt the pain of a body slamming into hers and driving her into the ground. Shrapnel exploded all around as a shield covered her body. And a pair of eerie light eyes glared into hers. Eyes she knew as well as her own.

Eve of Destruction.

Evie of Salvation.

The one and only person in her life who'd never failed her.

Her precious big sister and the last member of her family who wasn't dead. Rising to her feet, Eve dragged Jayne with her and shook her.

"What the hell, Jayne?" Those clipped words were even more rattling than the near miss.

Even so, Jayne couldn't speak. Not at the moment. She was too glad to see Eve alive and whole.

She'd been so sure that her sister had died a few moments ago when the structure shielding her had been blown apart.

But she should have known better.

No one was a better survivor than Eve.

Shadows played in her sister's eyes that mirrored her own horror and misery. "Get your skinny ass behind me. Now! Fall in line!"

Jayne obeyed out of habit. It was why her sister was a commander at the tender age of twenty-one. She'd risen up through their military ranks faster than anyone in Hyshian history. Her military prowess was without equal. Eve's intellect was off the charts and her skills far beyond her years.

But then they'd been forced to survive and thrive in conditions no one should endure.

Eve grabbed her. "Are your wings injured?"

Jayne's eyes bugged at a shouted question they were never supposed to speak about. "No."

"Then you need to unfurl them and get out of here."

Was Eve out of her mind? "Not without you!" Unlike her, Eve hadn't inherited the recessive gene of their family that gave Jayne a set of wings she could hide beneath her skin.

3

And Jayne wasn't strong enough yet to carry both of them out of this hell.

Eve shot and killed an enemy over Jayne's shoulder. "Don't worry about me. I can take care of myself, but not if I'm worried about you. Get to safety. Now!"

While Jayne believed that, she wasn't willing to abandon the last member of her family. That wasn't what Erixours did. It wasn't what they'd been taught.

"No!"

Eve growled at her. "You stubborn little bitch!" She fired more rounds. Clicking the mic in her ear on, she glared at Jayne. "Tweedle? I need you to turn around and—"

"Ah, hell no, Evie. I just got clear of that shithole. And not by a lot. By the yactos. And I mean the yacto of the yacto . . . of the molecule of a yacto. Are you out of your luna mind, woman?"

"Jed, turn it around or so help me I will skin every piece of you raw the next time I see you. Now!"

He cursed over their comm-links. "Why do you hate me so much?"

"Because you're one of only two males alive who hasn't disappointed me. Now move it!"

Tweedle cursed again.

Jayne laughed in spite of the hell raining down on them.

But really, this wasn't funny. "You'll be behind me?"

"I'm not going to die and leave you alone. You get into enough shit with me here. I cringe to think of the trouble you'd find without me."

Kissing her sister's cheek, Jayne unfurled her wings and took off.

But not before she heard the most precious words from her sister's lips. "I'm getting you out of this life, little bit, if it's the last thing I do."

Chapter One

FOUR YEARS LATER

J ayne sighed heavily as she waited for Eve to arrive. Heartbroken, she read back over her rejection.

So much for getting herself out of this wretched life . . .

So much for dreams.

She should have known better. Luck had never been her friend and her family was absolutely cursed.

Sitting down, she stared at the bottle of Tondarion Fire with lust and craving. More tempted than she ought to be, she refused to go there. Alcohol had ruined her father.

It'd ruined their childhoods and she wasn't going to succumb to those demons.

"I'm creating my own."

And she was, sadly. Maybe that was the curse of life. Period. Either you repeated the demons you knew were bad, or you summoned all news ones to come and torture you.

Why make more for herself when so many were already alive and well in her gene pool?

Just as she was about to give in, her door opened without preamble and Eve rushed toward her.

Her sister's light eyes were full of sympathy as Eve pulled her in for a tight hug. "I'm so sorry."

Jayne nodded. "Me, too. It was the last school I applied to. No one wants me."

"I want you." Eve tightened the grip she had on her. "It's not fair or right!"

She appreciated her sister's righteous anger on her behalf, but it changed nothing. "When has life ever been fair to us?"

Eve pulled back and wiped the tears from Jayne's eyes. "The day it sent Jinx to me."

Okay, she'd give Eve that. But really? Throwing a high-ranking League assassin into her life who could be killed for even speaking to her sister wasn't exactly a bene they should count.

It, too, seemed more like a curse.

While she loved Jinx, she, like Eve, was well aware of the dangers involved with having a relationship with one of the League's soldiers. Assassins were strictly hands-off.

The only way out for an assassin was death.

And still nothing could keep Jinx from protecting them. From loving her sister and doing anything for her.

Especially not something as trivial and rare as common sense.

"Why are we cursed?"

Eve shook her head. "We're not cursed."

Jayne scoffed. What else was it? Everyone in their family failed.

Everyone.

Their father had been driven into crime because everything he tried had blown up in his face. Everything. All their mother had wanted was a family. First, her mother had lost her fertility, then she'd lost her life to a rare disease that had come afterwards because she'd lost her fertility.

Double, undeserved whammy.

Eve had never wanted to be a mercenary. She'd dreamed of a simple life with a good man by her side. A techspert. That had been her sister's calling. Only Eve had seen herself in an office, not in her constant life-and-death escapades with an assassin and a crew of mercenaries.

Most of all, her sister had wanted children and given her life and Jinx's it was impossible.

And her . . .

Jayne had dreamed of being an elementary school teacher. Being around kids and watching them learn.

Simple things.

All denied to them. No one in their family had ever attained their dreams, no matter how small. Not since the day they'd been declared outlaws on their home planet over a genetic fluke none of them had asked for.

Though to be fair, there was a bright sparkle in Eve's eyes now that hadn't been there before. Jinx had at least lifted Eve up to where she was no longer as cynical and jaded as she'd been before he'd come along.

Jayne envied her that.

"It'll be okay, little bit."

She nodded, even though she didn't feel it or believe her sister's words. There was no need in making Eve feel bad while she was trying to help. "What do I do now?"

"You're welcome to continue on with my crew."

Awesome.

Mercenary work and bounty hunting. The last thing she'd ever wanted. Honestly, she was tired of trying to find easier ways to get blood out of her clothes. Clean the skin and gore from beneath her fingernails.

Packing weapons in concealed places on her body because every shadow was a possible threat.

Simple life. That was her ever elusive dream.

With a ragged breath, Jayne forced away her sadness. There was nothing to be done.

This was their family's legacy.

Humiliation and gore.

Resigning herself to her fate, Jayne drew a ragged breath. "Any new assignments?"

"An easy one just came in. I was going to turn it down, but . . ."

Jayne sighed in resignation. "How gross is it?"

"No blood for once." Eve pulled her comm out of her pocket and took a second to load her files. "Prince retrieval."

She scowled. "What?"

Eve handed her the comm link. "He's a runaway and his family wants him back."

That seemed uncharacteristically easy. "Don't they have security to track him down?"

Eve shrugged. "Some reason they're outsourcing." She jutted her chin toward the comm in Jayne's hand. "For that amount of creds, I'm not asking any questions."

Since when?

"Who are you and what have you done with my sister?"

"Ha, ha." Eve rolled her eyes. "Stop being dense. Do you want it or not?"

Jayne looked over it and realized Eve was right. Simple assignment. Grab an aristo and get paid enough money that she could have a nice retail therapy session to assuage her bruised dreams and self-esteem. "Sure. Why not?"

"Awesome. I'll get you signed up for it."

* * *

Alexios Hadrian Vicarius Scalera stood in front of the sink filled with dishes and cursed his very existence.

Gah, could I hate my life more?

Sadly, the answer was probably yes, but still . . .

No wonder he stayed pissed off all the time. At himself, his brother, and the minsid fate that had dumped him into this existence and then turned its back on him and his.

His boss glared at him. "What are you waiting for, dipshit?"

You to die and put me out of my misery? Biting that comment back, Hadrian ground his teeth as he fought the urge to splinter the bastard against the nearest wall, which would be so incredibly easy for him to do. But those kind of anger-management issues were what had caused him to be dumped here.

After a scalding lecture from his brother. *Never expose your fucking powers! Are you trying to get yourself killed?*

Most days that answer was no. But the fury that stayed with him was a serious threat to those who crossed him.

And this arrogant prick had no clue how close to death he trod.

Instead of punching him like he wanted, Hadrian slid his gaze to the asshole who owned the restaurant where he worked— not because he wanted this insufferable job, but because Isak was the only one willing to pay him hard creds under the table and ask no questions.

"I'm waiting for you to repair the bot that washes these."

Isak clapped him on the back. "That would be you, Vicar. Get started."

Don't hit him . . . Hadrian didn't know what he

hated more. This mess or that stupid nickname he'd given up by accident. He'd been using an alias that was completely unrelated to any of his numerous real names.

But the moment Isak had asked, Vicar had slipped out. Damn his brother for that ridiculous moniker that only Nero used.

Now he was stuck with it.

Well at least you didn't say Hady.

Yeah, he hated that one more.

Irritated beyond belief, he waited for Isak to vanish. Then he glanced around to make sure he was alone.

Yep . . .

"Want your dishes done, bitch?" He snapped his fingers and they were in place, washed and dried.

His brother would kill him if he ever saw him use his powers in public like this. Never mind for something so trivial.

But he wasn't about to waste what little youth he had left doing anything so distasteful, even if it did give him a low-grade headache to use his powers to do it.

Gah, Hadrian was so sick of hiding and being told what to do. How to live . . .

He wanted his life with no overlord suppressing him.

Don't be stupid. You tap your powers, and you can die. You don't ever know who's around you or what they can detect.

Live like a regular human, Vicar, or you'll die like everyone else in our family.

Painfully and in misery.

Nero had said that to him so often that it was permanently running through his head. In truth, he was surprised his brother hadn't tattooed it across his forehead.

Seriously though? What kind of trouble could he

find on this backwater hole where Nero had dumped him?

I should leave and not look back.

'Course that would only work until Nero tracked him down and kicked his ass, then dragged him off to an even worse, more remote hellhole. A lesson he'd learned long ago.

Big brother didn't play. Nero had risked his own life to save his when their planet had been destroyed by war and their race hunted to the brink of extinction. For saving Hadrian's toddler ass when Nero had still been a boy too young to witness the carnage, he owed his brother and would do anything for him.

Yet Nero still thought of him as that helpless toddler.

Even though Hadrian was better trained than his brother and as capable as any soldier, Nero wouldn't let up or give in.

He was the only family Nero had left and big brother hen intended to sit on him until he hatched.

Or went crazy.

It might be too late for the crazy part . . .

The buzzer sounded.

Great. They needed help up front. The only thing he hated more than washing dishes . . .

Facing the derelicts who drifted in.

With a low growl in his throat, he headed for the door.

Then froze.

For a full minute he couldn't breathe as he saw the woman at the counter. Tall, athletic, and surrounded by an air that said she was no one's prey or plaything, she had to be the sexiest thing he'd ever laid eyes on.

Long, thick black hair was pulled back from her pulchritudinous face in a tight ponytail. Even from here he could see her silvery blue eyes that were a stark contrast for her raven hair.

He didn't need his Trisani powers or instincts to know that she was a creature of complete and utter violence. No, he could see the way she watched the doors and everyone around her.

Fully alert.

Fully armed.

Like a predator on the prowl. She was just biding her time in case she needed to attack or defend.

Damn.

But with that came a heavy wave of caution. Was she after him?

So many had tried . . .

Watch your ass, boy.

"Vicar!"

Isak's sharp call reminded him what he was supposed to be doing.

Grabbing an e-pad, he headed for her before anyone else beat him to it. If she was an enemy, he needed to keep her close. "Your tablet's broken."

She scowled at him. And the moment those eyes turned up toward him, he was lost in the hidden pain he saw there. The shadows that haunted her soul deep. "Pardon?"

It took him a second to register her word. He jerked his chin toward the filthy e-pad in front of her. "That one doesn't work. You'll need this to place an order." He handed her his pad and felt the softness of her fingers as they brushed against his.

"Vicar!"

Wanting to trip Izak with his powers, he forced himself to behave. If she was a mercenary or assassin, the last thing he needed was to expose himself.

Please don't be someone I have to kill.

For one thing, he was really tired of people coming at his back. For another . . .

She was the epitome of what he'd wanted so long that he'd almost forgotten the sensation. Tough, beautiful. Confident.

And from the looks of her, capable.

Don't be another disappointment. "Enter point-oh-six under waiter and I'll bring your order to you."

"Thanks."

Inclining his head to her, he went to get the orders that were piling up and take them to their designated tables. But he made sure to keep his eye on her.

Not just because she could be threat, but because he wanted her to be no one important.

Except someone who could be important to him.

* * *

Jayne frowned as she watched her gorgeous waiter set a black backpack down behind the counter she was facing, and leave.

It can't be this easy.

Her luck never was.

Yet he matched the photo and description of her target. Exceptionally tall, lean muscles . . .

And insanely handsome.

Yeah, okay, that last bit hadn't been part of his description, but she'd noted it as soon as his photo had come over with the warrant.

In all honesty, that photo didn't do him justice. It had failed to capture the mischievous light in his blue eyes. The intelligence. Or the quirk to his lips as if he had a secret he was keeping from everyone.

His long brown hair was held back from his face in a shoulder-length ponytail that would normally have turned her off. Yet he made that look work.

Shabby elegance.

Sadly, looks like his weren't the norm. They were as rare as a smile on her face.

Not to mention, there was no missing the regal aura that clung to him like skin. That slow loping grace. What was it with the aristos that they all had the same carriage and deliberate mannerisms? Like it was genetically encoded in them.

And her target stood out in this filthy diner where most of the waitstaff and clientele hadn't bathed in a few . . .

Millennia.

Yeah. Breeding like his was a definite gimme.

Jayne flipped to her comm, which had a photo of a younger version of the waiter.

Definitely him. But why would a rich aristo be working in such a grimy shithole? This was a far cry the playboy vacation spots they normally frequented.

Then again, rich people did weird things all the time. Eve had found them in some of the most unlikely places imaginable. Weird fetishes.

Some just wanted the thrill of slumming-it.

Thankfully her sister's freakishly accurate facial cog program had found him here. When it came to tech, there were few people in the universe better than Eve, especially since her system was augmented with an illegal League feed courtesy of Jinx.

And you almost ignored it . . .

Jayne glanced around the filthy dive hole. *Of course, I did.* The only thing she could imagine wanting to vacation here was a cockroach.

Still baffled by it all, she reviewed the contract she'd signed to return him to his family. Maybe she'd misread something. But as she reviewed it, she realized that it'd been updated over the last few hours.

This was no longer a simple retrieval.

Alexios Hadrian Vicarius Scalera.

Spill-kill.

Her heart stopped at that brutal order that must have come through when they saw that someone had signed on to take the contract.

"What the hell?" The issuer had paid to have him killed in the most vicious way possible. They didn't just want him dead. They wanted him tortured first and then brutally executed.

What had he done?

Why would anyone hate him that much?

While it wasn't uncommon for someone to change a warrant once it was assigned, they were normally much subtler than this. More money. Bonus pay if you delivered something the issuer wanted.

But to sucker someone in for a minor retrieval warrant and then change it to brutal execution . . .

That was rarely done. Mostly because retrieving and executing were two different skill sets and those, like her, who retrieved didn't normally want to kill.

She looked up at him as he dropped off two plates at a nearby table. Unlike his mannerisms, his clothes didn't look regal. They were ragged. Worn-out. Even his shoes were scuffed from age.

He seemed so . . .

Normal.

Looks are deceiving.

She knew that better than anyone. It was something her sister used against many of her targets. Eve waltzed in looking like a seductive vamp, not the ruthless mercenary of legend, Eve of Destruction, then cut the heart out of those who thought her a harmless plaything.

Still . . .

In spite of his unbelievable height, her target appeared young. Not much older than her, if any. Too young for such a horrific sentence.

Your job isn't to question.

That was what her sister would say. They were mercenaries. *Do the job. Do it quick. Get paid.*

No prey. No pay.

But she wasn't Eve. She couldn't compartmentalize brutality the same way her sister did.

Sure, she could take a life if someone tried to kill her. That was one thing.

To take a random life for payment . . .

She wasn't that cold-blooded, and she didn't want to be. Honestly, she had a hard time reconciling the loving sister she knew with the vicious killer Eve could be.

But she'd taken out the contract. Once accepted, it was hers.

Either kill or be killed.

If Jayne failed to carry it out, two more assassins would be assigned. One to kill him.

One to kill her.

What do I do?

Jayne had just switched her comm so that she could message her sister when a shadow fell over her screen. Ready to battle, she looked up to find her target in front of her.

"Having trouble with the menu?"

She shook her head. "Texting my sister."

"Ah. I'll leave you to it. Let me know if you have any questions. I'd avoid the seafood. Beef . . . basically any meat. Unless you're Andarion or Phrixian. Those bastards can eat anything."

"Vicar! Get your ass over here!"

Jayne ground her teeth. Great. Another asshole who hated Andarions. Figured. It was why she and Eve were always so careful to make sure no one knew they had a drop of Andarion in them.

It never boded well for them whenever people learned of their grandmother's legacy.

Jayne watched him head toward a human who began yelling at him for dawdling.

Okay . . . a prince who worked at a dingy, backwater hole and allowed peasants to scream and berate him, without punishment.

One using a pseudonym. With a Spill-Kill warrant.

Something wasn't adding up.

But before she could consider it any further, she saw the guy on her right draw a weapon.

There was no missing the bloodlust in his eyes as he took aim for her target.

What the minsid hell?

It was her target!

Without thinking, she pulled her own blaster. "Drop it!"

The assassin turned toward her, then shifted his scope at her head.

Just as Eve had taught her, she shot first and without hesitation. The recoil reverberated through her as her mark rang true . . . right between his eyes.

One shot. One kill.

No questions.

Pandemonium erupted all around them. People and aliens screamed and ran for the door.

Except the owner and her target.

Her target watched her warily as he moved toward the bar where he'd dropped his backpack. The owner was too busy screaming about the damage, blood, and carnage.

Jayne ignored them as she made her way to the other

assassin and knelt by his side. Making sure to keep her weapon angled on him, she checked for a pulse.

He was dead.

But one could never be too careful.

She rifled through his pockets until she found his comm. It was still on the same page she'd been reviewing.

The warrant for *her* target.

She saw Hadrian's eyes widen as he realized what she was looking at.

Then his gaze went to the assassin's blaster that lay between them.

"Don't," she warned.

Before he could move, three people rushed into the diner, weapons ready.

At first, she assumed they were local law enforcement.

Wrong.

They looked at the man at her feet, then opened fire. Not just at her target, but at her.

Cursing, Jayne sprang into action. She started for the blaster, but it flew from the floor, into her target's hand at the same time his backpack flew from where he'd dropped it behind the counter.

She barely had time to register that before she fired at the newcomers and moved to shield her target.

Hadrian paused before he killed the woman who'd been at his counter, along with the ones shooting at him.

As she'd done a moment before and for reasons he couldn't fathom, she was protecting him from the others.

Stunned, he shrugged his backpack on.

Kill her. Don't risk it.

That instinct was ingrained in him. Nero would

have his ass for hesitating. Everyone was an enemy and no one could be trusted. If his life had taught him nothing else, it'd taught him that.

Trust is for the stupid and those who have nothing to lose. And it cost our family everything.

For all he knew, she was a Metamoran or a Chiller, or something a lot worse . . .

She grabbed the front of his shirt and yanked him forward. "C'mon. I have a transport out back."

He didn't move at first.

Not until she shot a blast past his shoulder and killed another assassin.

"Dumbass! Do. You. Want. To. Die?"

Her angry staccato words broke through his haze. Not that he was worried about dying. At least not here. Or now. But he was curious about her. "Lead the way."

With a quick jerk of her chin, she headed for the kitchen.

"Backdoor's–"

She shot it open before he could finish telling her Isak kept it padlocked. Guess his boss didn't count on that.

With an irritated grimace, she glared at him. "Could you move any slower?"

Honestly? Yes.

He didn't know what to say as she reloaded while he moved past her.

She growled at him. "Transport. There. Move like your life's at stake and people are shooting at us!"

"I'm going."

"Little faster, punk'n."

Her impatience amused him.

The number of assassins after them didn't. He'd barely crossed the alley, shrugged his backpack off his shoulders and got into the small, rusted out piece of shit before two shots hit it. "You sure this is safe?"

Sliding in, she glared at him, then floored it and ran over the alien who was shooting.

Guess it's safer than being outside while she's driving . . . He cringed at the sound of bones crunching, then barely caught himself as she swerved and sent him careening almost into her seat. "Who taught you to drive?"

"No one." She shot out the window.

"Are you licensed?"

"Not on this planet."

Awesome.

Hadrian cringed as they brushed against another vehicle, then almost hit a pedestrian who made the mistake of stepping out a door as they careened by.

On the sidewalk.

He clutched his backpack to his chest. "Where are we going?"

"Preferably where no one is shooting at us." She slammed on the brakes.

He hit the windshield and cursed. "What are you—"

"Sh!" She gestured up. "Drone," she mouthed the word at him.

Grinding his teeth, he looked up and saw it. Then did the stupidest thing he could . . .

He exploded it with his powers.

Jayne sucked her breath in as she watched the sparks rain down over the hood of her stolen transport. Granted, she'd suspected his race when he'd taken the blaster without touching it and summoned his backpack during the fight, but things had been happening so fast that she'd hoped she'd imagined that.

There was no mistaking this.

"You're Trisani."

He didn't say a word as he met her gaze. His eyes glowed with an unmistakable sheen that betrayed the heritage of a race that had been hunted to the brink of extinction.

Shit.

There was nothing she could do. If a Trisani wanted someone dead, they could implode a brain inside a skull. Cause a heart attack. Literally wish someone dead and they'd die.

Trisani were *the* assassins to beat all assassins.

No other race had ever been able to stand against them. Not without severe tech to dampen their psionic abilities.

Which meant that he already knew everything about her. He knew her thoughts better than she did.

Double shit . . .

Instinctively, she held her hands up. "I'm not going to hurt you."

"Why did you save me?"

Jayne froze at that question. Then she remembered his earlier one. "Don't you know why?"

He narrowed his gaze.

Her jaw went slack as the answer dawned on her. "You can't read my mind, can you?"

Hadrian tightened his grip on his backpack as she realized the one thing that he'd learned once they were free of other people. After he should have had absolute clarity and space to know every voice in her head.

Every doubt. Every fear.

Instead of those obnoxious intrusions he hated that usually overran his own thoughts, he'd heard nothing.

Not a single whisper from her, and that was highly disturbing. Abnormal. Only his brother had the ability to shield his thoughts from him like that.

But never had a stranger done this before.

It was something Nero had warned him about. Rare, and almost impossible and unheard of. Those tiny handful of creatures they couldn't read. *Clusas.*

Yet Hadrian had never met one before. He'd believed them to be some other form of gremlin Nero had made up to frighten him with.

Apparently, they were real.

And she was one of them.

Figured.

He unclenched his teeth. "I don't have to read your mind to kill you. So, answer my question."

"I didn't come here to hurt you."

"Then what do you want?"

"My warrant was only to return you to your family."

There was one problem with that. "My family's dead." And the sole member who wasn't, knew exactly where he was as he'd dumped him here to keep him "safe." So, there was no way in hell that Nero had sent someone else after him.

Never mind taken out a warrant.

That's the dumbest fucking system I've ever heard of. Leave it to the barbarians to come up with it.

He could always count on Nero to be succinct . . .

And bitter.

"Not according to the warrant I signed. Your family wants you back." Jayne glanced around the street before she turned the transport off the main road. "Look, let me take you to my sister and we can sort this out."

Hadrian reached for the handle.

"You won't get far out there on your own."

That was what she thought. "You'd be amazed at what I can do."

She let out a short laugh. "I'm sure you're right. Trisani are known for being amazing." Smiling, she swept a glance over him that affected him in a way it shouldn't. Not to mention the damn inconvenient timing of his body craving a woman that had been sent after him. He had to pull his thoughts back before they got him into some serious trouble.

"Name's Jayne . . . Erixour. We both know you can melt my brain so why not stay here for a few and let's find out what's going on, okay?"

As bad as he hated to admit it, she was right. He could kill her with nothing more than a sneeze.

Granted using his powers for something like that would take him down a day, maybe two, but she didn't know that. No one knew how much using their powers cost them. It wasn't exactly something they bragged about.

Or broadcast as it was a weakness they guarded with their lives. And no two Trisani were ever affected the same way.

Some weren't affected at all.

Right now, his head was killing him from that damn drone, grabbing the blaster, and doing those dishes.

If he'd had any idea he was going to be attacked, he'd have never used his powers so carelessly for a menial chore.

In all honesty, he needed a nap to recover.

Damn Nero for being right. It'd been stupid to use his powers for something so trivial. Served him right.

But this was life and death.

Depending on what he had to do to survive, he could easily go down and be at their mercy. And the saddest part? He wouldn't know what pushed him over the edge. Sometimes he could use his powers and it would cost him nothing.

Other times . . .

He could do something simple and pass out. Nero claimed it was because he was young.

Hadrian didn't know the truth. He only knew the reality that seriously sucked.

Debating what to do, he studied Jayne. Physically, she appeared around his age.

But there was an air to her that said she'd lived beyond her years. A hardness that came from experiences someone their age shouldn't have.

It was why he hated to look in a mirror. All he saw was an old man who'd been kicked since the day his brother had saved his life when Hadrian was toddler.

Had she wanted to hurt you, she wouldn't have saved you.

That seemed logical. But people were just so damn treacherous that logic seldom seemed to apply. End of the day, they were lying minsid snipes who seemed to get their jollies by causing as much mental pain to someone as they could.

If she was one of those . . .

He'd kill her as a public service.

Hadrian let go of the handle. "All right. I'll stay . . . for a minute. You betray me . . ."

"You'll kill me. I get it." She started the transport again.

Still not sure of her intentions, he adjusted the backpack in his lap. "You really didn't take a kill warrant?"

"No." She jerked her chin at the small bag she'd put on the seat between them. "You can look at my original contract and see."

Hesitant, he reached inside her pouch and pulled out her comm. "Code?"

She placed her finger against the screen.

It lit up to show him a screen full of junk he couldn't read. "Trade license," she said as she swung the transport toward the nearest landing bay.

Finally, the screen showed him a signed warrant that was written in Universal.

Hadrian scanned her contract. She was right. All she'd signed on to do was take him in. "You're a licensed bounder and *assassin*?"

"Yeah."

Interesting. Unless they were agents of the League, most assassins tended to be older. "Aren't you a little young for that?"

He didn't miss the pain that flashed in her eyes as she pulled her comm from his hand.

"That's none of your business."

"You're hunting me for someone who lied to get a warrant. That makes this all about me." He watched as she slid her comm back into her pouch.

"You have a point."

Yes, he did. But he also had another question for her. "So, what happens when your original contract gets flipped to a kill warrant?"

When she responded, her tone was flat and emotionless. "If I don't kill you, they'll kill me."

Made sense. Given what he knew about warrants, when one was assigned, the assassin either completed it or they were terminated.

She touched his arm. "But I'm not a killer."

"Yeah, right. I saw the body count in the diner and your license."

She cut a glare at him. "I'm a soldier, Hadrian. That license is to protect me from facing charges when I protect my own life and those I love. It's not the same as cold-blooded murder."

He wanted to argue, but she was right. He'd taken his own fair share of lives. Not because he'd wanted to.

Because he'd had no choice.

Kill or be killed.

The universe sucked and those who lived in it refused to let him live in peace, free of their meddling. Sooner or later, someone always came for him.

And honestly, it felt good to have someone call him by his real name for once. Not even Nero used it anymore for fear of someone overhearing it.

But how could he trust a licensed assassin who'd been sent after him?

As she said, if she didn't kill him, they would kill her.

Kill or be killed. In this world, it was that simple.

That harsh.

Her comm rang. She tapped her ear to answer the call. "Yeah?"

Unbeknownst to her, Hadrian could hear the feminine voice on the other end.

"Jaynie? You okay?"

"I'm fine."

"Where are you?"

Jayne glanced at him. "Where I wish I wasn't."

"Don't play evasive with me, you little bitch! Where are you?"

A tic started in her jaw. "I acquired the target someone told me would be easy-peasy. Neither of us is happy, thank you for asking. I'm heading to my—"

"Stop where you are. Now!"

"What?" Jayne slammed on brakes.

"Killamon just sent a group of his assholes after your target. I got the notice a few minutes ago. Stop in your tracks. He thinks you're me and tracked your fighter. They're waiting at the hangar to jump you and claim your target. Are you using the comm I gave you?"

"Yes."

"Okay. Find a hole and stay there. Jinx is en route, and I'm right behind him. Stay low until retrieval. We'll find you and get you out."

Hadrian watched as she tapped her ear and let out a disgusted sigh. "Well, that's just fucking awesome. Take this easy assignment, Jaynie," she mocked in falsetto. "You can do it in your sleep. No problem. Don't worry." She slammed her hand against the wheel. "Thanks a lot, you minsid harita!"

"Having a bad day?"

Jayne froze at that calm, dispassionate question. The fact that it came from her target succeeded in instantly calming her down. "Well, I guess it's not as bad as yours, is it?"

"Guess that depends."

"On?"

He inclined his head toward her side of the windshield. "Whether or not that bastard is accurate. And if he hits you before me."

She cursed as she saw the assassin targeting him. Without thinking, she hit the gas and ran straight for him.

The assassin's face paled as he shot his weapon, then turned to run.

Jayne had no mercy on him as she ran him over.

"Nice."

Glaring at him, she threw the transport in reverse and backed over the assassin. "Don't start with me. I'm in a bad mood."

"I can tell." Hadrian cringed at the additional bump as she went forward, and again ran over the assassin. "You know, I'd feel bad for that guy if I didn't know what a piece of shit he was, and the fact that he killed two children on his last mission."

"Bully for you." She hit the gas and headed down a side alley. "While you're crawling through people's heads for information, you wouldn't happen to know a safe place to hide here, would you?"

"I would suggest the shithole where I live, but they've probably found it by now."

"Most likely. Any other shitholes you frequent?"

"Not really. I try to avoid shitholes as a rule. All-in-all my life is usually boring."

Once again, she slammed on the brakes and opened fire. "I wouldn't say that, punk'n. Looks pretty intense from the fifteen seconds I've known you."

"Well, aside from the occasional near-death visitation from one of your ilk ... it's pretty routine."

"Mmm. You don't say?" She reloaded and started down another side alley.

"I said it. Doesn't make it true." He winked at her. "Those are just the lies I keep telling myself in hopes they might one day come true. Sadly, running like this is my norm."

Jayne wasn't sure what to make of him and that blasé tone that defied the anger in his eyes. He hated all this as much as she did. "You're not what I was expecting."

"Really?"

"Yeah." She drove more sedately as she scanned the street for some safe place. "Figured you were another spoiled aristo taking a vacation on mommy and daddy's creds."

"Retrieved a lot of those, have you?"

"No. My sister has."

"Ah."

She scowled at him. "You always this stoic?"

"No. Sometimes I sleep."

For reasons she couldn't fathom, she found him strangely charming.

And that disturbed her. Because of her career that she hated, and the baggage she carried from her less than stellar childhood, she went out of her way to avoid men.

There was no need to even try to get involved with anyone. Who could look past the blood she kept on her hands? She wasn't some simple-minded fool who thought for one minute that a prince would come and save her.

No. Her past was too brutal for that.

Just look at Eve.

The last thing she wanted was to be in love with a man who could bring down the wrath of the League on her back.

And the men her career brought her into contact with . . .

She was better off alone.

Jayne saw Hadrian eyeing her blaster on the seat between them. "You have any weapons?"

"Just my charming wit, and devilish good looks."

Some places, that was all he'd need. Sadly, this wasn't one of them.

Except for . . .

"Well, from what I saw you do earlier with your wit . . . it's pretty lethal."

He clicked his tongue and winked. "True. Being Trisani doesn't suck, and I still have the blaster I confiscated from our friend at the diner. And my two daggers."

"Really?"

Hadrian nodded. "You always have two hidden weapons."

He was right about that. "One for them to find."

"And one to keep."

Jayne gave him props for being well-trained. "I'll remember that you know that."

"Ditto."

She swerved to miss some trash and a homeless woman who was sleeping next to it. "So why a hit on you this big? Who'd you piss off?"

He shrugged. "Don't know. I try to keep to myself. All I can figure is that I'm Trisani."

Which in and of itself made him one hell of a target. "But how many know that?"

"No one. It's not how I open conversations and those who would know me are no longer in this plane of existence."

She handed him her link again. "Do you know who issued the warrant? They claim to be your uncle."

He scrolled through the screen until he saw the name. "Never heard of an Anicetus. No idea who it could be."

"Well, we need to ditch the transport." Jayne swung into an alley and quickly turned it off. She grabbed her things, got out, and waited for Hadrian.

He'd just joined her when she felt a presence behind her.

Jayne moved to attack, but before she could identify who was after them, Hadrian threw his hand out.

She felt the blast from his hand ripple through the air around her like an electrical current. It raised the hair on her arms.

That wasn't the impressive part.

The fact that it lifted their assailant up and slammed in into a wall was.

And he wasn't the only one.

Two more snipers fell from locations she hadn't detected.

Damn . . . she never wanted to be on the receiving end of *that*. "Impressive."

Hadrian didn't speak as he hissed and staggered against the transport.

"You okay?" Jayne rushed to his side.

His nose was bleeding, and she didn't miss the way his hands trembled.

Shaking his head as if to clear it, he clutched his

backpack to him. "We have to get out of here. I won't be conscious much longer."

Shit.

That was all she needed. While she wasn't the tiniest woman around, he was gigantic. Few men towered over her.

Sadly, he was one of them.

"All right. Let's find someplace to lie low."

Wiping at his forehead, he led her toward another transport.

"What are you doing?" she asked.

He shook his head and widened his eyes as if struggling to stay conscious. "There's another landing bay. Small, out of the way dock."

She was confused. "Okay."

"I have a fighter there for emergencies."

"Why didn't you say so?"

"Didn't know if I could trust you."

"So, you trust me now?"

He scoffed as he opened the transport and tossed his backpack in. "Have no choice."

She watched the way he moved. He was really unsteady. "Should you be driving?"

"No." He got into the driver's seat anyway.

Awesome. A sane person would leave him to it. Too bad her sanity had died a tragic death years ago when she'd run bank jobs with her father.

Not to mention the fact that sanity didn't really run deep in the roots of her family tree anyway.

Erixours were known for other gifts. Not for being reasonable or mentally stable. That had been bred out of them generations ago and they tended to revel in their lunacy.

She slid into the passenger seat as Hadrian started

the transport. "What happens if you pass out before we get there?"

"Guess we'll both die."

She scowled at that uncalled for response. "I really don't like you."

He grinned as he swung them toward the street. "Too bad. I think you're adorable."

Jayne froze at those unexpected words.

Was he serious?

More to the point, was he flirting? She had so little experience with that side of life, that she had no idea.

But her sister had told her all kinds of shit that men had pulled on Eve to try and get her in their beds.

Men could be creative, she'd give them that.

"You know it's a myth."

He scowled. "What?"

"Putting a woman in danger and it causing her hormones to surge and make her horny. Really, it just pisses us off."

He laughed a rich, unexpected sound unlike anything she'd ever heard. Damn, he was incredibly handsome. His smile was absolutely devastating. "I'll try and keep that in mind." Then he winced and wiped at the blood coming from his nose.

Jayne realized that he was in a lot of pain and doing his best to hide it. That was something she understood more than she wanted to.

Never let anyone know your weakness. Show nothing to the world and they can't use it to harm you.

Anger swelled inside her at the memory of her father's words. No one should be taught such a harsh lesson before they were old enough to attend school.

Obviously, Hadrian had been tutored on the same plan that had made her the monster she was.

Reaching into her bag, she pulled out a tissue.

"Here."

He did a double take before he took it from her. No doubt kindness from others was as foreign to him as it was to her. "Thanks."

As he drove, she realized that the assassins had backed off. No one was taking aim at them, and she couldn't see anyone following their transport. "Did we lose our assholes?"

"Not really. I'm using powers I shouldn't be to avoid them and shield us."

Impressive. She wished she had that ability. It would make her life so much easier. "Can you feel them?"

"Oh yeah." The way he said that was actually comical.

"What does it feel like?"

"A thousand tiny pissants in my brain."

She laughed at his dry tone. "Literally or figuratively?"

"Both." He swung the transport unexpectedly.

In that moment, she understood how he'd felt earlier when she'd been behind the wheel. "Gah, no wonder people bitch about my driving. I get it now."

He didn't comment as he pulled to a screeching stop next to a worn-out building that looked as if it should have been condemned a decade or so ago. It even came with a passed-out hobo asleep under some trash.

At least she hoped he was asleep. From the looks of the poor man, he could very well be dead.

Hadrian paused next to him.

Frowning, she thought he might actually be rolling the poor soul until she saw him tuck a handful of creds into the man's jacket before he led her toward an antique slide-door.

She didn't know why, but the way he'd done that

33

touched her. As if it was an automatic habit he didn't even think twice about.

Whereas most people would have walked right past the man without a second glance, Hadrian, who was running for his life, had taken a few seconds to care for someone else.

That was so effing rare.

And it shouldn't be. It said a lot about him.

He opened the door, then looked back to wait for her and scan the street. "Shouldn't you be moving like your life is at stake?"

Ignoring his dig at the hell she'd given him earlier, Jayne glanced about nervously. "Are they after us?"

"Not yet."

She ducked inside the filthy hangar that was infested with vermin. Cringing, she kicked an oversized rat out of her way.

There wasn't a single vessel here that appeared space worthy. Everything around them was rusted out junk that she wouldn't even use for spare parts.

"Please tell me this is a joke."

An irritating grin curved his lips as he headed toward a particularly nasty looking craft. "What? You turning craven?"

Her stomach sank. "I'm not getting into *that*."

He tsked . . .

And walked past it.

With an infectious laugh, he headed for a door that held a hand-scanner. She watched as he placed his hand on the pad and it unlocked the door that slid open to reveal his fighter.

Relief poured over her as she saw a modest, but safe and clean alternative docked inside.

"You're such an asshole."

The humor died on his face as he staggered.

"Hadrian?"

He covered his eye with his hand. "I won't last much longer." Hissing, he made his way to the fighter and unlocked it. His breathing heavy, he helped her up the ladder, then climbed in behind her.

"Here." He handed her the lock-key drive.

Jayne plugged it in while he strapped in behind her.

Reaching around her seat, Hadrian entered the launch code and fired the engines. "Can you fly this?"

She took a second to go over the controls. They were different from her ship, but basically the same. Everything was set up backwards from her ship. Otherwise, it was fairly standard. Controls were controls. "Yes."

"Good." He barely spoke that word before he fell unconscious against her seat.

And not just a little bit. He was out in a way that was actually scary.

Wow. Closing the canopy, Jayne put his headset on and prepared the launch. The good and bad thing about where he was docked was that there was no controller. No one to grant any permissions or stop her from leaving. No records being kept about who came and went. But that meant that she had to watch for any and all traffic on her own, and she had no idea how fast this ship was.

In fact, she had never even seen one like it.

Biting her lip, she hesitated. Given that Hadrian was hiding and hunted, it would most likely be fast.

"All right. We can do this." She took the controls and did her best to ease it up.

It rocketed out.

Fast was an understatement. At the rate it shot forward, it would take her stomach a week or two to catch up. Good news, they would definitely outrun anything sent after them.

Bad news, she couldn't really read the nav on it. Or any of the computer systems, for that matter.

"Where the hell am I going?"

She wasn't even sure of the language or alphabet. "Really? Why isn't this in Universal?"

Because he's hiding . . .

He wouldn't want anyone to be able to see where he'd been or locate his name, or any identifying information.

Damn it.

The ship shot through the atmosphere in record time and so smoothly that she barely felt the burn of it. Impressive. Someone had modified the drive to something the likes of which she'd never seen or felt– which made sense given that the Trisani were the ones who'd invented FTL drives and space travel to begin with. It was stunning tech. But since she couldn't read the heading or settings, she had no way to reset anything, or know exactly what she was doing.

Seriously, what the minsid hell?

How could she fly like this?

She didn't dare try to reset anything for fear of hitting the wrong thing and ejecting them into space or shutting down life support and not being able to reactivate it.

She needed help.

"Let this work." She dialed out on her comm.

Nothing went through.

Of course not. There was nothing to relay the signal to without a hookup and she couldn't read his schematics to make the right connection.

Damn.

"Fine." She dialed Jinx. Since he was League, she wouldn't need long range capabilities to pick up his frequency. He could always answer.

"Shadowborne. Go."

Jayne let out a relieved breath. "Hey. Do you know what frequency this is?"

"Jaynie?"

"Yeah." She rolled her eyes at the fact that her voice was so similar to her sister's that not even Jinx could tell them apart.

"Where are you?"

"Hadrian's fighter. I launched it but can't read the nav on it. I have no idea where I'm heading." She took a picture of the console and sent it to him. "Have you ever seen anything like this?"

He ignored her question, probably because the pic hadn't arrived yet. "Why did you leave the planet? I'm only a few minutes out."

"It was too thick, even with my skills. They massed out the contract and everyone was hunting him. Hadrian took me to his fighter. We thought it was the best course of action to get the Tophet out of there."

"Where's your target now?"

"Unconscious, in the seat behind me."

"Well, that's useless."

"Not funny."

Jinx didn't respond. He was good at ignoring conversation he didn't like and even better at dodging questions. "I just got the photo."

"And?"

"Looks like an ancient Trisani script."

She ground her teeth. "I was afraid you might say that. Can you read it?"

"No. Your sister's the only one I know who knows any Tris."

Of course, she was. "So, you have nothing useful to tell me on how to pilot this thing."

"Best advice? Don't hit anything. And you're right. It is an open contract. Vicious one."

She cursed as he used his League magic to confirm what she already knew.

Open contracts were so rare as to be virtually non-existent. The League almost never granted one because it could lead to assassin guilds fighting over a single bounty, and that could lead to all-out war. Which was the last thing the League, or anyone else wanted.

A contract was only deemed "open" until an assassin signed their name to it. Then that specific assassin was given a specified amount of time to complete it.

If they failed to kill their target during the allotted time and were still alive when it ended, the League took out its own kill contract for the assassin who failed their mission, and the original contract was opened again for another to take and complete.

If the assassin died in pursuit of their target, the contract was immediately opened for someone else to sign, and usually the League added more creds to it as they didn't want anyone that dangerous left on the streets.

If the kill-warrant target terminated more than two professional assassins who'd signed on, the League then sent in their own.

That was where soldiers like Jinx came in.

Fast, brutal.

Inescapable.

No one survived being hunted by a League assassin.

No one.

Jinx snorted. "Obviously, they bribed the right person. My higher-ups are corrupt as shit. You know that."

Yes, she did. The League Prime Commander had it in for Jinx and had almost slaughtered him a year ago. It was how he'd met her sister.

But that didn't change the fact that this was wrong.

"We can't kill him, Jinx."

"If you can't, then you have to hand him over to me and let me finish this."

"No. It's bullshit."

"Jayne . . . be reasonable."

"It's a life, Jinx."

"It's a target. An assignment. Nothing more."

She would never understand how her sister and Jinx could do that. Just look at someone and cross them off a list as a commodity.

"Listen to me, little sister, it's his life or yours and I'm more attached to you. The League will take you both and you know it. He's assigned a death warrant. There's no way out for him. And if you're there when it happens, they'll take you, too. You know how this plays out. Turn on your tracker and make this easy."

That would be the smart thing.

However . . .

"There has to be another option."

"Jayne!"

"Give me another alternative, Jinx. I mean it!"

Cursing her under his breath, he let out a tired sigh. "There's only one other way. Find the asshole who took out the warrant and get them to rescind it."

"Can they do that?"

"Yes. But they never do."

"But they could."

"And we could be eaten by a giant lava monster, Jayne. Actually, you'd have better luck being eaten by a giant lava monster."

"You're not funny."

"No, I'm realistic. Comes with the assassin uniform and tattoo. And you need to be also. Life is harsh and you don't need me to tell you that. You've lived as much awful as I have. Think about it, Jayne. Do you really think that asshole in the backseat would spare your life?"

Probably not. No one had ever shown her any mercy.

If she'd learned anything in her handful of years, it was that no one other than her sister could be trusted. Honestly, she didn't even trust Jinx.

Not entirely.

Everyone betrayed. It was the one thing in life that she could depend on. The one absolute constant besides death.

People were always looking out for their own best interests. They didn't care who they hurt.

Or how badly.

That was the saddest part of humanity.

When she was a child, her own father had sold her out to lessen his jail sentence. He'd traded her freedom for his own and had been fine with it.

That had been the harshest lesson of all, and it still burned inside her with an unforgiving fury. Even though he'd been dead for years, it wasn't dead enough.

Not after everything he'd done to her and Eve.

Some things just couldn't be forgiven.

Your brother never betrayed you . . .

No. He'd spent his handful of years trying to protect her. And Sway had died before he'd had a chance to really live. A chance to grow old.

But in a weird way, she viewed that as the greatest betrayal of all. He'd left her to this life.

Had abandoned her just as her father and mother had.

For that, she hated him at times.

How could you, Sway?

"Jayne?"

"I won't do it, Jinx." *I won't be like everyone else. Someone has to do the right thing.*

Just once.

40

"Damn it!"

She cut the transmission. Right or wrong, she wasn't going to be what life kept trying to make her.

Heartless. Bitter. Vindictive.

You won't take my soul. I won't let you. .

It was the only thing she had left. They'd stolen everything else from her long ago. Her childhood. Her innocence.

Her sense of fair play.

Her family.

What was left?

A hallow shell of the woman she'd wanted to be. A ghost who struggled to feel anything other than despair and misery.

Every day when she woke up, she had to struggle to find a reason to get out of bed and keep trying. A reason to not let the darkness have her.

I'm such an idiot.

Risking her life for someone who didn't care anything about her. Someone who'd probably kill her and leave her in a ditch. This had to be the dumbest thing she'd ever done. And given all the idiocy she'd committed . . .

It said a lot.

But at the end of the day, she had to live with herself. There was no escaping that face in the mirror. Just as there were lines that shouldn't be crossed.

Lines that once crossed would forever turn her into the monsters of her past.

I will not lose my soul. She kept repeating that. She had to.

Tears gathered as she remembered the first time she'd taken a life.

The sick gleam in the bastard's eyes as he'd come for her. Oh, he'd deserved it, all right. He'd been intent on raping her and leaving her for dead. Had laughed at her pain and would have harmed who knew how many more had she not stopped him.

Still . . .

That look in his eyes as his life had faded. It haunted her to this day.

Two people die when you take your first life. The one you kill and the person you used to be.

No truer words had ever been spoken. And there was no going back.

Life had pushed her down paths she'd never wanted to travel. It kept shoving her where she didn't want to go.

"Why *do* I keep fighting?"

Maybe Jinx was right. It would be easier to just hand Hadrian over and let the assassin do his job. She'd get paid and be free to live her life without being hunted.

Biting her lip, she looked down at the bounty on her comm. It was a shit-ton of creds.

It'd pay off every bit of her debt. Leave her flush for the next couple of years.

Hell, she'd even be able to go to school if she could find one that would let her in.

All you have to do is kill an innocent man.

It was that easy.

More than that, it was her job.

He's asleep. He won't even know . . .

Chapter Two

Hadrian came awake to a massive headache. At first, he thought he was at home, until he heard the hum of his engines and remembered what had happened.

He sat up fast and banged his head against the fighter's canopy. Cursing, he realized too late that he'd crawled into the backseat where it was much lower.

"You okay?"

"Not really." He was pretty sure he'd just given himself a concussion. "Where are we?"

"No idea."

Hadrian yawned at Jayne's overly calm words. "What?"

"I said I could fly it. Never said I could navigate an alphabet you didn't forewarn me about, punk'n."

Oh. That had been done intentionally to keep others from stealing is ship. And to prevent her from taking him in to the League. But he wasn't about to tell her that. "Guess I should have switched it over."

"That would have been nice."

"How long was I out?"

"Long enough that I need a bathroom. And I'm really hoping this red light isn't your fuel gauge."

That made his heart stop as he scrambled to see past her seat.

Jayne enjoyed the panic on Hadrian's face as he quickly went over their settings. She knew it wasn't the fuel, but it was nice to get a little payback on him for the discomfort she felt.

He let out a sigh of relief. "It's the dampeners."

"What I figured. Just messing with you."

Growling at her, he flipped a switch near her hand that turned her instruments into Universal. "There's a planet an hour away with an outpost. Can you make it that far?"

"Do I have a choice?"

"Not unless you want me to jettison you."

She gave him an arch stare. "Be kind of hard since you'd go with me."

He snorted. "You seriously overestimate my survival instincts when up against my aversion to bodily fluids."

Jayne laughed at his unexpected retort. "You're seriously not right, are you?"

"No. I'm not. I'm completely fucked in the head. I have a death warrant I don't deserve. An overprotective brother who is insane on his best day. A woman I don't know about to piss in the only thing I own, and everything else I can claim fits into a backpack I have to carry with me everywhere I go because I never know when I have to hit the ground running. In what world would any of that make someone normal?"

He was right. And she couldn't blame him.

She smiled sadly. "Sorry."

"No worries. Could be worse."

"Yeah. We could both be lying on the floor of your diner."

"Or *much* worse. You could have ordered Izak's steak."

44

Jayne snorted. How pathetic that that was what it really came down to. A good day was one where she didn't bleed. A better one was a day where she didn't make someone else bleed more.

And the best days were when her sister came home alive and unharmed.

Sad, truly. It seemed like there should be more to life. A better reward for trying to be a good person.

She sighed heavily at just how pathetic it all was. "So, who's this fighter registered to, anyway?" She knew it couldn't be under his name, given his family lineage and how long he appeared to have been running.

"Does it matter?"

Not really, but she was curious who might come looking for him. "I can pull the reg."

"Derring Orrin."

That was weird. "Any particular reason you chose a cartoon character?"

"It has absolutely no relation or bearing on my real name. And if anyone looked it up, they'd be blitzed with a zillion thousand results that have nothing to do with any real living person."

Made sense. It was actually brilliant given what he faced.

"So, what happens if you're asked for ID?"

He handed her his comm.

She glanced at it, then laughed. It was a photo of him wearing glasses . . .

With the name Derring Orrin. That picture looked nothing like the adorable rogue she'd found. He was definitely a creature of many facets.

Still laughing, she handed it back. "Nice forgery."

"I have several." Of course, he would.

"Your brother?"

He narrowed his gaze on her. "Why would I tell you?"

"Because I'm flying your ship?"

"That gets you my respect. Not any names."

He was smart and quick. She liked that in a person. It wasn't often anyone could keep up with her.

"Fine. Be that way. I have secrets, too, you know."

Hadrian felt a corner of his mouth lift at her petulant tone. He had no reason to be amused by her and yet he was.

She's after your head.

Yeah, but she'd saved his life.

Don't trust her. You can't afford to be that stupid.

Trust was for imbeciles. People lied and they deceived. His entire family had been slaughtered by one single betrayer they'd made the mistake of letting into their lives. His entire race had been brought down by their own.

For no real reason. Petty jealousies. In-fighting and just plain stupidity.

Worse? The ones who'd sought the destruction of his planet had destroyed themselves in the process. No one had won.

Maybe it was karma.

Or just plain sick.

But it had taught him one thing. In a game of war, the best option was to avoid it. Everyone got dirty in a fight, and no one walked away uninjured.

The only thing it showed was the ones who were willing to bleed with and for you. It culled the pretenders from the herd so that you knew just how rare true loyalty actually was.

"So . . ." He leaned forward to check their heading. "What's our plan?"

"Get to a bathroom, then find out who's after you and get your contract canceled."

"That a thing?"

"It's what I was told." She handed him her comm. "Are you sure you've never heard of the person who opened the contract on you?"

He reviewed the contract again. Anicetus Scalera . . . While Scalera was his father's surname, he'd never heard Nero mention an Anicetus before. "I don't recall anyone by that name."

"You sure?"

"Yeah. All my family's dead." He said automatically. Besides, he definitely didn't have any uncles who'd survived the war. "Long gone."

"Then why would someone pretend to be a member of your family?"

"Given the fact that we're Tris and in hiding . . . your guess is as good as mine. I can't imagine anyone who survived the war would ever be stupid enough to contact the League for a contract." Not with the number of people who wanted to enslave their handful of survivors.

"What about your brother?"

"He's not out taking contracts against my life. Trust me. If he wanted me dead, he'd do it himself and bury my body where it wouldn't be found."

"You're sure about that?"

"Positive. He knows all the best hidey-holes."

Snorting, she rolled her eyes. "Not what I meant. You sure you can trust him?"

"Yeah." Nero was the only one he trusted. "So . . . we have to find a bathroom, shelter, weapons, and some asshole pretending to be my relative."

"How do you know they're pretending? You and your brother survived. What makes you so sure someone else didn't, too?"

She had a point. He could cede that to her, however

47

. . . "Pretty sure if one did, they wouldn't be so keen on killing me."

"Why?"

"No reason to. I'm not the heir. My brother is. Why get rid of me while he's still alive?" Not that anyone could inherit the throne of a dead nation. "Besides, why bother?"

Jayne paused at that. He was right. That wouldn't make any logical sense.

Trisa was a fallen empire that had been split up and divided among human races. The people living there now would have no loyalty, or any reason to reestablish the royal house they'd overthrown.

"What other enemies do you have?"

"I don't. Never stay around any one place long enough to make any. For that matter, no one knows my real name. Never mind the names of my dead relatives."

Yet they'd taken out a warrant while pretending to be his uncle. "You sure?"

She could feel the withering stare he was giving her. "Yeah. Positive. I know what info I let out."

"You talk in your sleep?"

"Wouldn't matter. I don't close my eyes around strangers."

She arched a brow at that.

"Rare exception."

For some reason, that thrilled her. It was rare to meet a guy that good-looking who wasn't a man-whore. One who didn't trade on his looks.

Yeah, but it's not like he has a choice.

True. There was no telling what he'd have been like had he not been forced to lie low for the whole of his life.

Jayne took her comm back and stared at the warrant. "This is hopeless. We'll never figure out who did this."

"Don't be so sure about that. I think I know someone who could be helpful."

$$Chapter\ Three$$

J ayne paused as Hadrian led her into what had to be the shadiest looking dive she'd ever seen. And she should know given that her father had a penchant for hanging out with the sleaziest, most disgusting creatures that had ever belly-crawled out from the primordial ooze.

Her father, Egarious Toole, would have loved this place. He'd have been right at home with the card sharps on her left and the alcoholics at the bar. But it would have been the prostitutes he'd have gone home with, provided the drug dealers didn't get to him first and sell him something that would have left him unconscious, on the bathroom floor.

She winced at childhood memories neither she nor her sister could quite purge. There were just some images of parents no child should carry.

Her father half-naked and covered in his own filth was definitely one of them.

'Course hers were mild given that Hadrian would have witnessed the massacre of his. All things considered, she was lucky. When her father had finally died from his excess, she'd seen it coming for years and hadn't been there for the grand finale.

Still, it had hurt. But once the initial shock had passed, it'd been a relief to not have to deal with his drama anymore.

At least that was what she told herself.

In reality, he'd still been her father and a part of her had loved him. Had wanted him to be the father she'd deserved and not the broken man the universe, rough circumstances, and bad luck had made him.

As she swept her gaze around the crowded room, she tapped Hadrian's arm. "Thank the gods you let me stop and use the restroom on that outpost. I shudder at what the ones here must look like."

Hadrian laughed. "Yeah. Even I wouldn't try for it, and I don't have to squat." He paused at the bar.

A gnarly orange-skinned alien appeared. "What can I get you?"

Jayne didn't hesitate with her order. "Dysentery on tap with a wedge of salmonella. Maybe a side of tetanus."

This time, Hadrian laughed out loud.

The alien bartender wasn't so amused. "You ordering or just going to insult my place?"

"Neither." Hadrian held up a wad of creds. "Tell Sheridan the favor he owes his cellie has come due."

The bartender scowled at the money. "He's liable to toss that in my face."

"He won't."

"He does and I'm coming back and kicking your scrawny ass."

Jayne didn't speak as he ambled off. "You sure about this?"

"Nope. This guy . . . he really is liable to shoot us. According to my brother, he's a cantankerous ass."

"Just what we need. More shots to dodge." Shaking her head, she moved to stand by his side so that she could scan the crowd. Hadrian looked so out of place. "Then again, we're lucky no one's shot at us yet."

"Meaning?"

"You look like an uptight Enforcer and I look like my sister. I'm surprised they let us in. Even more surprised they haven't thrown us out."

"Because no one's looking at me."

Jayne glanced around and realized he was right. "You expending more powers?"

"Yes, and it's making me sick to my stomach."

"Careful with that. You pass out and I might leave you here."

"Chance I'm willing to take."

She was about to comment when the surly bartender returned. "He'll see you."

Without another word, he led them through the crowd to a small room in back.

Jayne wasn't sure what to expect until she stepped into a shabby, dingy room where an interesting Ritadarion sat in front of an expensive computer set up that no one would have ever attributed to such a rank establishment.

Handsome as the devil himself and with eyes blacker than space, the man had a military grade computer that belied his rebel clothing.

She should have known . . .

C.I. Syn. *The* go-to techspert in the universe. This man was a legend. Everyone in their line of work knew him or knew of him.

Syn met her gaze first and scowled, then he looked to Hadrian. "What the hell is this?"

Hadrian put his hands in his pockets. "I have someone I need you to trace."

Suspicion crept into Syn's eyes. "Haven't you heard? I'm retired."

Hadrian let out a derisive snort as he swept his gaze over the expensive tech setup. "You don't look retired."

"What? This?" Syn gestured at his gear. "Hobby."

Jayne scoffed. "Some hobby."

Syn shrugged, nonchalantly. "Keeps me out of trouble."

"And it means that you can run a trace."

Syn growled at Hadrian's persistence. "Nero know?"

"Above his paygrade."

Syn snorted. "Nothing is above his paygrade where you're concerned. You trying to get us killed?"

"I'm trusting you on this."

That garnered a full laugh. "I don't keep secrets from your brother. I can't."

"Yeah . . . he's a massive pain in the ass that way. Can you at least avoid him for a bit?"

Syn scratched at his cheek. "Can try. But like you, he has a nasty way of tracking me down." He shifted his gaze back to Jayne. "I don't even want to know why *you're* here. Eddon on a ladder, you two are going to get me mutilated, aren't you?"

Hadrian scowled. "What do you mean?"

"You know who her sister is, right?"

He shook his head.

Syn laughed even harder. "Damn . . . You want to tell him, Jaynie? And how is it possible that you don't know, Hady?"

Hadrian screwed his face up. "Stop with that name. I hate you both. As for the other . . . can't read her. Wish I could say the same for you, buddy. Your head's a mess."

"Always." Syn held up his bottle of cheap alcohol. "Why I drink."

Hadrian turned toward Jayne. "Eve of Destruction? Seriously? *That's* the sister you keep going on about?"

Ouch. He really could read Syn's thoughts. Until then, she hadn't realized just how lucky she was to remain silent where he was concerned. Apparently, he really could pull all thoughts from someone's head.

"Yeah." She winked at him. "Still think your brother's the bigger pain?"

"He can read my thoughts if I let my guard down . . . what do you think?"

"That would suck worse."

Syn shook his head. "Try being in the same room with the two of them. You feel butt-ass naked."

"That, I am familiar with. Jinx and Eve have the same effect when they start cross-examining me on where I've been or what I'm about to do."

Syn nodded. "Yeah, I can see where that would a wreck a day."

"And your balls." Jayne crossed her arms. "So, miracle Syn, what can you tell us about who took the contract out on our boy here?"

One dark eyebrow shot north as Syn realized why they were there. "Who did what?"

Jayne held her comm up so that he could read the warrant. "Someone's pretending to be his blood. I'm assuming you're the one who scrubbed Hadrian's past. So, you probably know his history better than anyone."

"'Deed I do." He took her link and studied it. Then let out a low whistle as he stared at Hadrian. "Nero know about this?"

"No idea. I just learned about it . . ." He glanced at Jayne. "What? Ten, eleven hours ago?"

She checked her watch. "Yeah, that's about the time we met under a hail of blaster recoil."

Syn reached for his drink and took a gulp. "Can't do this sober. Shit!" Rubbing his eye, he started typing.

Jayne picked up a white lab coat from the chair nearest her. It actually had a real medical badge on it with Syn's photo.

But not his name. "Dr. Sheridan Belask?"

Syn sucked his breath in sharply as he jerked it from her hands. "Don't be nosing around my stuff."

"I hope this is a joke?"

Disgruntled, he folded it away. "My day job."

She glanced to the bottle of almost empty alcohol next to his hand. "I hope you practice a little more self-restraint when the lives of others depend on you."

"Sadly, I do. Though to be honest, they'd probably be better off if I drank." He returned to his keyboard. "My thoughts are much clearer when my demons are pickled."

Scowling, Jayne crossed her arms over her chest. "So . . . how does a tech thief end up in med school?"

Syn laughed. "That's a long and complicated story. While interesting, it's not one I'm drunk enough yet to share."

Dang it! She really wanted an answer. But she knew enough about him to know he wasn't about to divulge anything he didn't want to.

Jayne moved to read over his shoulder. Then realized that, like Hadrian, he used an alphabet she'd never seen before. "What is it with you guys refusing to use Universal?"

"Keeps my passwords safe." Syn sat back as something scrolled across his screen. "This is so weird."

"I know."

He rolled his eyes at Hadrian's droll tone. "No. There's no one alive who knows you survived."

She scoffed. "Last time I checked, I still had a heartbeat, champ. And so do you."

Syn shook his head. "Not what I mean, Jayne. As

55

you said, I wiped him clean. As far as the universe is concerned, he died on Trisa with the rest of his family. There is literally no trace of Hadrian Scalera, anywhere. You, me, and Nero are it for those who could identify him. Until . . ." He threw a photo up on the wall. "Someone got this picture of you, Hadrian. Do you recognize it?"

Hadrian shook his head. "No, but I'd say it's about a year ago."

Jayne frowned. "How do you know?"

"The background. It's a Caronese city. Wasn't there long . . . maybe two months. About a year ago."

Syn studied the angle of it. "Who took the picture?"

Hadrian shrugged. "I've never seen it before, and I am not one to pose for anyone. I know better."

Jayne considered that. "Old girlfriend?"

"Don't have one."

"Boyfriend?" she tried again.

"Don't have one." He gave her a droll stare. "Running every few months doesn't leave much time for a personal life. Nor is it conducive to telling anyone anything about myself, such as my real name."

"Looks like it came from a closed circuit city camera." Syn turned back to look at them. "So, I suppose our question is . . . who has Nero pissed off?"

Chapter Four

Hadrian scowled at Syn. "Why would Nero have anything to do with someone wanting me dead?"

"Well, if *you* haven't pissed off anyone and no one knows your real name . . . what's left?"

"Someone trying to get back at your brother." Jayne passed a sympathetic stare to Hadrian. "It tracks."

Hadrian scoffed. "Nero would never tell anyone about me. *He* knows better."

Syn arched a brow.

"You don't count."

"Uh, ouch." Syn took a drink.

"You know what I mean, Sheridan. You're the only person alive he trusts and it's only because of the history you two have and the fact he had to trust you to survive. He would never put my life in the hands of anyone else. He's too paranoid for that."

"You're not wrong. But someone learned about you, somehow. And we know your family's dead."

"Do we?" Jayne asked.

Syn nodded at her. "There's no doubt. Nero saw their parents die. Their brother Trajen and sister Julia escaped together, but had they lived, they'd have been in touch by now. No blip of either of them has ever been found and I do look from time to time. For Nero's sake. He blames himself for what happened to them." And if Syn looked for someone, it was like League assassin level of tracking.

No one escaped him.

Hadrian let out a slow sigh. "Just leaves Auggi."

"And Ani."

Hadrian scowled at the name he didn't know. "Ani?"

"Anicetus."

His heart skipped a beat at Syn's answer. "The person who took out the warrant? I thought it was my uncle who had that name."

Syn shook his head. "Yes and no. You had an older uncle, but I'm thinking that this one was meant to be your eldest brother who died before you were born."

Hadrian gaped in shock. "What?"

"Didn't you ever wonder why there was such a big age gap between Nero and Augustan?"

Hadrian winced. Yeah, the thought had crossed his mind as the rest of them had been born no more than two years apart.

What Syn said made sense. There was enough gap in Nero and Auggie's ages to have had a child perfectly placed like the rest of them.

Syn patted him on the back. "Nero doesn't really talk about it because he was insanely close to Ani and he still feels that burn." He jerked his chin toward the screen. "I'm thinking whatever sick psycho took out this hit picked Ani because of that. And they did it to really hurt your brother. No other reason."

Which meant they had to be close to Nero to know something that Nero had kept from him.

Jayne cocked her head. "What about this Auggie?"

Syn shook his head. "Nero sent him after Hadrian

the night everything blew. He was gunned down before he could get Hadrian out. Again, Nero watched it happen and barely got to Hadrian before he was killed, too."

"How old was he?"

"They were all kids when it happened. Hadrian was still a toddler."

But she could tell from the expression on his face that Hadrian was haunted by it. How could he be otherwise? "I'm so sorry."

"It's okay. I don't really remember much. Just the screams and the fear, and Nero holding me so tight that I thought I'd suffocate. My brother still has nightmares . . . and still holds onto me so tight that I feel like I'm suffocating." Hadrian might be trying to make it sound light, but the pain in his eyes was haunting.

"Yes, he does." Syn saluted them with his bottle. "And judging by his late-night screams, his are as relentless as mine. Don't envy him that."

Those words piqued her interest. "Just how close are the two of you?"

"We shared a cell in prison."

Jayne covered her ears and backed up. "No. No. No. Not another fucking word!"

Hadrian was stunned by her uncharacteristic response, and the paleness of her features. She was genuinely terrified as she began pacing and panting.

This was a full-blown panic attack.

"She hasn't been out long," Syn explained. "Apparently, her nightmares are still with her, too."

Holy shit. Hadrian widened his eyes. "What'd you do?"

"Not a damn thing!" she growled as she struggled to control her rapid breathing.

"Truth." Syn inclined his head. "All political bullshit

that had nothing to do with any action Jaynie had taken. It was all done to hurt her sister."

Hadrian felt those words like a fist to his stomach. From the stories his brother had told, he knew the horrors Jayne had faced in jail. She was too young for such.

Then again, Nero and Syn had been, too. It was why they remained close. Syn had been a child, put there for what his father had done and for discovering a secret that could bring down the assholes in charge.

No other reason.

Nero had been locked up because he'd been born of a race everyone feared. No one had known what to do with him as they tried to groom him into a political weapon.

All bullshit.

Had Syn not been there, Nero would never have survived.

There was no justice in this world. They all knew it. Every one of them had been slammed down by injustice from the moment they'd drawn their first breaths and hadn't been smart enough to strangle themselves with their umbilical cords.

Pain, misery, injustice, and poverty seemed to be the only thing any of them could count on.

Oh wait, he forgot the one biggie. The humdinger that was always hovering over all of them . . .

Betrayal.

Yeah, that petty bitch loved to rear her head up whenever one of them was stupid enough to let down their guard.

What hurt the most was the fact that none of them trusted easily. They knew the sting of betrayal too badly. Yet somehow, they'd all succumbed to it in spite of their common sense and survival instincts.

Syn was right.

"It should be easy to find out who if they're trying to hurt Nero. That's a short ass list."

"Yeah, it's basically confined to me."

Jayne took another step back.

Hadrian snorted. "But I know it's not you."

Syn winked at him. "Yeah. 'Cause I'd have to be terminally stupid given the ease your brother walks through my head."

That made her feel a little better. Maybe. "Any way you can trace it?"

Syn shook his head. "Jinx could do this easier than I can. He has clearance with the League databases. I'd have to breach them."

All well and good, except for one minor detail. "We're not exactly talking at the moment."

"Why?"

She inclined her head to Hadrian. "He wants me to put a blast through Hadrian's head. I refused."

"Good call. 'Cause Nero is an enemy no one wants. Not even Jinx is that good and none of us need your sister going after Nero. There's a scenario made for a horror movie." Syn glanced down at his computer. "Give me an hour and let me see what I can dig up. I might have a way to find out something."

She sighed. "One hour. You got it."

Without a second glance, she led Hadrian back into the crowded bar where discordant music thumped so hard, it felt like a second heartbeat. How could her sister listen to this?

If Hadrian still had his headache, he had to be in agony.

She looked back to see him scowling at the mural on the wall where the club had its name painted, alone with demons rising out of the letters.

He cocked a brow at her. "Devil's Vein?"

"Yeah, they always come up with something weird. Don't they?" She winked at him.

"Hey!"

Hadrian ignored the shout, assuming it was for someone else. At least until a huge hulking beast of a man rushed Jayne.

He grabbed her by the throat and slammed her against the wall. "You fucking slut! You killed my brother!"

That brought him back to the present. With his own feral curse, he grabbed the asshole, pulled him away from Jayne, and slugged him hard. "Leave her alone."

He started for Hadrian, until he noticed his size. That caused him to back up and reevaluate how much he wanted to bleed tonight.

Hadrian put his body between the man and Jayne.

Instead of taking another punch, the nasty bastard spat on the ground at Jayne's feet. "I hope an assassin puts a blast right between your eyes, you bitch!"

That just made Hadrian all the madder as the man's real thoughts bombarded him. Those images . . .

Uh-huh. Without hesitation, he grabbed the asshole by his shirt collar and dragged him to stand in front of Jayne. "She's not Eve Erixour, you stupid bastard. Apologize for attacking an innocent woman."

The man paled considerably. "W-what?"

"You heard me. Apologize or I'll give you a taste of what you wanted to do to her."

Eyes bulging, he swallowed with a loud gulp. "I'm sorry."

"Yeah, you are." Hadrian slung him so hard against the wall, it knocked him unconscious. Still unappeased, he moved to Jayne as she wiped the blood from her lips. "You okay?"

"Another day in paradise."

Disgusted at the truth in that statement, he cupped her chin his hand so that he could inspect the damage. "Do people always mistake you for your sister?"

Jayne was stunned by his care. "As I said earlier, it happens."

"Doesn't make it right."

"Sadly, it doesn't make it lethal, either."

He scowled at those words. "You have a death wish?"

"Most days."

That was something he could relate to. And he hated that fact. But this was not how he wanted to live and every time he thought about the future . . .

It was a struggle not to end it all.

After all, what was the point? What did he have to look forward to? He didn't dare allow anyone to get to know the real him. He'd never be able to have kids. A career.

Not even a home or pet.

Nothing that couldn't fit in his pockets or backpack.

Gah, he hated what his life had become. What it'd always been. "Guess we need to find someplace a little less crowded."

Jayne nodded even though she had no idea where to go. She glanced back at her unconscious attacker. Part of her felt like she should be pissed at Hadrian for thinking her unable to tend her own messes. But the other part of her was happy to have someone rise to her defense.

Not that Eve or Jinx wouldn't have done the same. And just as quickly.

But . . .

This was different. She wasn't used to a stranger being pissed off on her behalf or jumping in to defend her. Like Hadrian, her life wasn't conducive to letting others in.

Wasn't even really conducive to sanity. Nothing ever made any real sense to her. So many bad memories she wished she could purge.

In fact, she couldn't even recall the last time she'd had a happy memory.

How sad that she woke up each day, praying it would be a normal, uneventful day. Or her last. Just seeking a moment of quiet.

How sad that it never came true. That she just kept living, even though she had no idea why. And she kept getting hammered by a life that seemed to resent her trying to live it.

She was too young to be this tired.

Hadrian paused to stare at her. "Do you know how disturbing it is for me to be around you and have no idea what you're thinking?"

"Not really. Happens to me all the time."

Laughing, he shook his head as they left the club.

"Besides, you're not missing much. My thoughts are usually morose. Honestly, I don't want to hear them."

He snorted. "I relate." Hadrian paused to survey the dark street. "So, where to, my lady?"

"Hell in a handbasket." She glanced around for cameras or other surveillance. "Failing that, somewhere other than the corner of Pain and Suffering. Should we try for all-out misery?"

He let out a long sigh. "You have the strangest sense of humor."

"Yet I attract you. Hmmm."

He didn't comment. Mostly because it was disturbingly true. And she didn't need to know just how attracted he was to her. "You hungry?"

"Always."

"There's a diner on the corner."

"Goodie!" She held her fists up like an excited child. "Always wanted to die in a diner."

"You mean dine, right?"

"Sure. I like your optimism. I'll go with it. I wonder if the diner has failed the same exact health codes as the bar, or if they found new ways to make their clientele sick."

She was so strange . . .

Hadrian hesitated before he led her toward the restaurant. He'd never met anyone quite like her. 'Course this was probably the longest he'd ever spent with anyone other than Nero and his foster parents.

He flinched as he remembered their deaths. And all because they'd been Trisani, harboring one of their own. While he had no real memories about the deaths of his parents and siblings, he fully recalled the assassins that had found them.

The debt he and Nero owed them for hiding him so that he wouldn't be gutted, too.

Damn . . .

Everyone close to him died.

That was a fact that made him wonder if he hadn't been born cursed.

But at the moment, it was hard to consider himself cursed while standing next to the sexiest woman he'd ever seen. She was exquisite. Especially the way she walked.

Confident. Slow and seductive.

The funny part was that he knew she wasn't even aware of it. She wasn't paying any attention to the number of heads that turned her way. Or how people watched her.

She just was.

And she stirred thoughts in him that he knew better

than to have. Dangerous thoughts given his status and history.

Don't get involved with anyone. He could hear Nero in his head, shouting at him.

His brother was right, even though it galled him to admit it.

Trying his best not to think about that, he followed her into the diner.

There were several aliens who watched them with a gleam in their eyes that said they recognized her. Although, from their thoughts, he knew they, too, mistook her identity.

Poor Jayne.

He'd give her credit though. Jayne caught on to what they were doing. She eyed them as she walked slowly past their table, then took a seat so that she could keep them in her line of sight.

Then, he saw it. That same hopeless desperation that haunted him. It was plain and clear in her light eyes.

And it reached out to him as he understood better than he wanted to.

Hadrian didn't speak as the waitress came over. Not until Jayne ordered Tondarion Fire. "Make it two."

The fuchsia-skinned alien eyed them. "You got the money?"

Jayne reached for her pocket.

"I got this." He pulled out the creds and handed it to her. "Bring the bottle."

Jayne inclined her head. "Thank you."

"Anytime. After all, I owe you a bounty for not killing me."

She snorted. "True. You're worth a lot."

"Glad someone thinks so. My brother doesn't think I'm worth shit."

She wrinkled her nose. "He must think you're worth something to keep protecting you."

"I think that's more narcissism than anything."

"How so?"

"I die, he grows old alone."

Jayne paused at those words. "Yeah, I get it. Sucks to be hunted and have to hide who you really are."

"You can't imagine."

"Bet I can."

He quirked a brow at her. "Explain?"

"Ever heard of Winged Andrions?"

A time or two. Andarions were a strange, warring race who preyed on anyone dumb enough to get in their way . . . and rumors said that they hunted and ate humans for sport.

More than that though, they were known for their quirky family titles that they would fight to the death over. Being a rigid caste culture, Andarions valued the purity of their family bloodlines and race above all else. "That's a family title-thing, right?"

"Now, but it wasn't always so."

"What do you mean?"

She smirked at him. "Back in the day, the winged clans were named that because they were actually winged. As in they soared through the skies like birds."

"Seriously?"

She nodded slowly and pulled back from the table as the waitress delivered their drinks. She picked hers up and held it as if in a toast. "My grandmother was a Winged Batur."

He choked on his drink.

Jayne glanced around the bar before she did something that would make Eve go into conniptions. She unfurled her wings to their full impressive expanse.

Several patrons near them scurried away.

God, it felt good to let them out. It was something

she rarely did as it caused more questions than she wanted to answer.

About everything.

But what the hell?

With a relieved sigh, she stretched them wide before she tucked them back into her skin.

At least Hadrian had the good grace to look sheepish. "I am so sorry for my comment about Andarions."

She knocked her drink back in a single gulp. "You and everyone else." She wrinkled her nose. "For the record, it's why they allow the myths and bullshit to continue. Easier to go with it than try to educate others."

Hadrian held his hands up. "Honestly, I have nothing against any Andarion. But you have to admit, your people will eat just about anything."

Jayne rolled her eyes. "Not true. Andarions are actually very picky eaters."

"Never knew."

"Most don't bother to find out, either." She took another drink.

Hadrian heard the sad resignation in her voice. "Again, I relate. My entire race was eradicated for no other reason than mistrust and prejudice." Which burned all the more, given how much his race had contributed to the others.

His people were the ones who'd created the first space program that united their universe. All the main tech that was the backbone and science the others depended on wouldn't have ever existed but for the Trisani people.

Instead of thanking them, they'd annihilated them all, then rewritten history to take credit for all the innovations and discoveries the Trisani had made.

And that fury simmered deep inside him as perpetual hunger. A consuming hatred that had never stopped to think about other races that had also been hunted and hated.

That they, too, had been given a raw deal by fate and others.

Jayne snorted. "One fucking royal nut job went after every Fyreblood and Winged species and purged us. Believe me, I get it. To this day, if we're found, we can be executed. Neither Eve nor I will ever step foot in Andarion territory."

That he fully understood. And he hated the degree to which he related. No one should feel their pain.

He gestured toward her back with his glass. "That is really incredible, though."

"Not as good as being able to read someone's thoughts."

"That's true, but it's not as great as you think."

"How so?"

"Gives me a lot of migraines. And sometimes nose-bleeds. While it can save my life, it can also ruin it. Nothing like having someone smile and pretend to be friendly while they're calling you names in their head that you can hear."

Screwing her face up, she visually cringed. "I'm so grateful I have no idea what my sister really thinks of me. I have enough damage from what she says. I can only imagine how much worse it would be if I actually heard the unfiltered shit she pulls back from speaking."

"Yeah. No privacy."

"No betrayal."

He laughed bitterly at that. "You'd think that. Sadly, the truth is different. We still get sucker punched from time to time. People don't always think their treachery before they pull it, especially when they know you can hear their thoughts."

Wow. That was something she'd have never dreamed could happen to them. And it chilled her to the bone to think that people could be so vicious.

Not like you don't know that.

True. Whenever she thought nothing could shock her more, some asshole came out and sunk to an even lower level of dirtbag.

He inclined his head to her shoulder. "Does that hurt?"

"What?"

"Your wings when they come out. Do you feel it?"

"I do. The skin tingles before the wings appear. It's like having a limb fall asleep, then there's a pulling through it. But it's not really painful. Just itchy."

He took a second to consider that. "I had no idea your breed existed."

"You're not alone. Most non-Andarions know nothing about us. But that genetic defect is what cost most of my family their lives. So, I understand what you're feeling about being persecuted. And betrayed. A lot of Andarions turned us in and curried the favor the royal house by helping to purge us out of their society."

He held his glass up. "Here's to righteous anger."

"Here. Here." She clanked her glass against his. "May it continue to warm my blackened soul at night."

"Does it?"

Jayne drank the last before she answered. "No. There's nothing left to warm me, really."

Hadrian turned his glass over. "Cold to the deepest part of my being."

And that was the truth. He'd been guarding himself and his emotions so long that he really didn't feel things like others. He'd been forced to abandon his feelings. To bury them so deep that they were faint memories.

Until her.

She made him feel something else. Things he'd forgotten about.

Things that were dangerous as they could lead him to places he knew he shouldn't go.

Suddenly, his comm rang.

Nero. He was the only one who ever called.

This won't be pleasant. A part of him wanted to roll the call. But that would be a mistake as it would cause his brother to hunt him down immediately.

And kick his ass for worrying him.

Sighing heavily, he answered it. "Hi."

"What the fuck?"

Hadrian smiled at Jayne's shocked expression. Apparently, his brother's voice carried. "Nice to hear from you, too. Been what? Fifteen hours? I think that might be a record."

"Cut the shit, Hadrian. Are you safe?"

He ran his gaze over Jayne's heavily armed, sexy body. "That's a loaded question." She was dangerous to him in so many ways, but none of them in the way his brother meant. "But I'm not being physically threatened at the moment. No."

"Where are you?"

"Chasing down leads on who hates you."

That caused Nero to back down for a second. "Pardon?"

"Well, no one knows me enough to like me, never mind hate me so much that they'd take out a hit warrant to end my life. I'm not worth the expense. What do you need to tell me, big bruh?"

"You think this is my fault?"

"No. But you have a lot more enemies than I do. You actually socialize and kill people who probably have families that don't think too highly of you and would want to get back at you for what you did to their friends and family, by say . . . killing your little brother. Who would hate you enough to come at me?" Hadrian wasn't expecting an answer. He assumed Nero would be as clueless as he was.

So when his brother answered, he was floored.

"Mordacity."

"As in one who likes to bite?"

"No, dipshit. As in a caustic bitch . . . Mordacity Pride. She's an incee."

Slang for independent assassin.

Shit.

For a long, slow second Hadrian couldn't breathe. "You know who did this?"

"Of course, I do. I don't talk about you to anyone."

"Except a caustic bitch?" Nero's words, not his.

"I was wounded and delirious at the time and your name came up while I was out of it. I had her word that she'd never use it against me. A few weeks ago, she told me she'd get back at me for pulling away from her. But this . . . I'll kill her!" Nero broke off into a string of Trisani curses that Hadrian was glad Jayne couldn't hear or understand.

"Can you slow the profanity for a bit. You have a girlfriend?"

Nero finally took a breath. "No. I had a friend with benefits until she took a hit from me. We had a falling out over it."

"Enough that she's coming at me?"

"Apparently." Nero paused a second. "There's no one else who would know about you."

"Or about Anicetus?"

Nero hesitated before he answered. "Yeah."

Hadrian met Jayne's curious gaze. "Why didn't you tell me we had another sibling?"

"There was no need. You have enough people to

mourn. I didn't think adding one you never met would benefit you in any way."

Instead, Nero had mourned him in silence. Kept a piece of their family history from him. Maybe he should be mad or upset that Nero had done that.

But how could he?

Nero was protective to the end.

It was why Hadrian tolerated his brother on those days he wanted to strangle him. They had a shared pain that few could relate to.

Even so, Hadrian couldn't resist ribbing him. "After all the lectures to me about keeping my distance from everyone . . ." He tsked.

"You see why? Bad things happen when you invite others into your life. I fucked up and now you're the one—"

"I'm fine."

"Are you?"

"Well, aside from my mental and emotional scars, and the asshole I have for a big brother . . . yeah."

"You're not funny.

"I am honest."

Nero cursed again. "Where are you?"

"Someplace safe."

"Awesome. While you're there, can you find all my individual missing socks and the papers I lost two days ago?"

Hadrian rolled his eyes at his brother's warped sense of humor. "I'll keep my eyes peeled."

"You better keep your ass safe."

"That's the plan." He also planned to keep the woman with the finest ass he'd ever seen safe, too.

"Stay put. I'm on this and will be back as soon as I know something."

Hadrian clicked off the link and set it aside.

"Trouble at home?"

He snorted at Jayne's sarcastic question. "I'm always in trouble. I think he still considers me a three-year-old toddler."

"But does he cut your meat for you? My sister tries to do that for me to this day. First time I had a whole steak, I had no idea what to do with it."

Without warning, he felt a presence approaching. Before Syn was seen, he heard him.

Hadrian stood up and moved a third chair to their table.

Syn hesitated as he neared them. "I hate when you and Nero do that."

He laughed. "Can't help it."

Syn straddled the chair and put his arms over the back. "Have a nice nap?"

"Just fried our brains."

Ignoring Jayne's comment, Syn took the bottle that was on the table and read the label. "Ooo, good stuff." He uncorked the bottle and picked up Jayne's glass before pouring himself a liberal drink.

He knocked it back in one impressive gulp. "Ah!" Then he turned his attention to Hadrian. "I have a name."

"Mordacity Pride?"

"Stay out of my head!"

Hadrian smiled. "Didn't have to go there."

Syn scowled. "Don't fuck with the drunk guy. You never know how we'll react."

Laughing, Jayne scratched her cheek. "His brother just called. He must have told him."

"Then what did you need me for?"

Hadrian winked. "Comic relief."

"Ha ha." Syn made an obscene gesture at Hadrian. "Then can I crawl back into my hole?"

74

"Do you have an address?"

"For the hole where I live? None that I give out."

Hadrian snorted. "You know what I mean."

"Address, birth registration, permits. You name it, I found it."

Of course, he did. That was what Syn did best. Jayne would salute him with her drink, but he'd taken it from her and appeared to have no interest in returning it.

"Want to hand that address over, buddy?" Hadrian asked.

Syn poured himself more Tondarion Fire. "Not now."

"Pardon?"

"If Nero knows about this and her, we should let Nero handle it."

Hadrian pulled a small e-tablet out and began making a note. "All good. I have it. Your memory is impressive." He stood up.

Syn grabbed his arm. "No. No! Bad idea. Why would you leave good alcohol to go chasing down someone your brother will find first?"

"Personal satisfaction."

Syn scoffed. "Overrated."

"Then curiosity."

"Stupid reason." Syn rolled his eyes. "Besides you know what they say."

"Curiosity is the foundation of science?"

Syn let out a pain-filled noise. "Damn your Tris origins. Y'all take all the fun out of everything."

Hadrian clicked his tongue. "That's what they say." He met Jayne's gaze. "Ready?"

"Yeah, sure. Time to blow some shit up, kill a few enemies and get this party started."

Syn let out a disgusted sigh. "Fine. But I can't let you two go it alone."

Hadrian scowled. "Why?"

He gave them a droll stare. "Because I like my testicles. Not that I get to use them much, but still . . . the thought of Eve or Nero removing them from my body makes me cringe. Especially the manner in which they'd detach them. I have enough shit in my life. I don't need that, too."

Hadrian tucked his pad into his backpack. "Suit yourself, but my fighter only seats two and you're not pretty enough to sit in my lap." He grinned at Jayne. "You, I would let, though."

Those unexpected words stunned her past the ability to think of a witty comeback. "I'm not sitting in anyone's lap."

"Yeah!" Syn playfully slapped Hadrian's arm. "Have some home-training."

"How? That would imply that I once had a home."

Jayne paused at Hadrian's words. Though they were said as a jest, she understood the pain of surviving in a place and not having a home. Just a roof where you despised every fucking inch of it.

It was absolute misery. That isolation and longing. The bitterness.

That burning ache to be safe and protected. To have one person who wouldn't sacrifice you to save their own ass.

Even though she knew her sister and Jinx would kill to protect her, it didn't fill the void that was there from never having known safety as a child.

To know that any moment her entire life could be blown apart by the selfishness of someone else.

Even her own father.

Damn you, you sonofabitch . . .

She still wanted to find her father's remains and just

beat the shit out of him. She could only imagine how much repressed fury Hadrian hid. Hers simmered constantly in her soul like a shield volcano just waiting to burst forth and burn everything in its path.

Sense be damned.

It was what made her such a powerful warrior. That ability to tap the raw, unspent fury and unleash it against whoever was dumb enough to be in her path when it broke.

There was nothing like it.

And here they were . . .

About to depart on another journey into the unknown.

Syn glanced past them. "Sadly, I can't join you two personally. Can't take time off from the hospital. But . . ." He grinned at something over her head. "I summoned a backup."

Jayne turned to look behind her.

Her jaw went slack as she saw a huge Andarion male heading for them. She would say he was as wide as he was tall, but the beast was at least as tall as Hadrian, or taller. If he were that wide, he wouldn't be able to come through a normal doorway. Though to be honest, he did have to bend over to make it.

Damn.

His long, black braids were immaculately pulled back into a single ponytail. At his age, she'd expect him to be in their military, yet he wore civilian clothing.

And while it'd always bothered her whenever someone commented on her eye color or Eve's, she now understood why Andarion eyes were disconcerting. That pale white really stood out against his dark skin.

They alone would have made him appear feral and fierce. Combined with his fangs . . .

Full-blooded Andarions were scary creatures.

Hadrian straightened up slowly to face him. She was impressed that he met him as an equal. If he had any fear, he kept it completely concealed.

Syn grinned at her before he addressed them. "Hadrian meet Hauk."

Hauk inclined his head to Hadrian.

Hadrian just arched a brow. "He is definitely not going to fit in my fighter . . . even by himself."

Jayne laughed.

And so did Hauk. Shaking his head, he scowled at Syn. "These the two?"

"Yeah."

"Awesome." He swept his gaze from Hadrian to her and then paused. "Sorry. I don't mean to stare. You just remind me of someone."

"Friend?" she asked.

"Almost family. But she's Andarion."

Hadrian's frown deepened as he met Jayne's gaze. "Are you related to Galene Batur?"

She wasn't sure who was most stunned by the question. Her or Hauk.

"My cousin. Why?"

Hadrian clapped Hauk on the shoulder. "Explains why they favor."

At the offended look on Hauk's face, Hadrian's eyes widened. "Sorry. I forgot the no-touch Andarion rule."

Rolling his shoulder, Hauk stepped away from him and turned his attention to her. "You really Galene's cousin?"

Jayne braced herself and slid her hand toward her blaster. "Yeah. You have issue with the Winged Baturs?"

"No. Just wondering how she's been."

Jayne shrugged at the last thing she expected him to say. Relaxing, she moved her hand from her blaster. "Haven't seen her since I was a kid. We don't exactly stay in touch. Andarions have a natural dislike for half-breeds and that side of the family made it known a long time ago that they had no use for us."

He held his hands up. "I get it. I've flown through that animosity myself, but no worries from me. My best friend is mixed human and Andarion, and my brother married a human."

That caught her off-guard. "Seriously?"

Hauk made the Andarion sign of sincerity over his heart.

Syn took another drink. "And he's a War Hauk."

That caused her jaw to drop. War Hauk's were second only to their royal house when it came to the Andarion caste system. "And you're friends with mix-bloods?"

Hauk flashed her an adorable grin. "I've never done what was expected of me. Besides, I'm the last male standing in my branch after they disowned my brother for his marriage. They can't afford to disown me, too. Gives me a lot of latitude."

Yeah, right. Not from what she knew of her Andarion relatives. They were a mean lot when you displeased them. Most of her family wouldn't even acknowledge them. Even though she'd been exiled from Andaria, her grandmother had been considered dead by her family the moment she'd married a human.

But Jayne wouldn't hold that against Hauk. He seemed decent enough.

She met Syn's gaze. "You trust him?"

"With my life, which is what Eve and Nero will come for if anything happens to either of you."

"You're expanding, brother. Proud of you."

Syn snorted at Hadrian's comment. "Don't be. I'm still not sure I'll survive this. Guess it's a good thing I don't like living, anyway."

Hauk shook his head. "So, I'm just basically their guard lorina?"

"Yep. Make sure no one messes with them."

He saluted Syn before he turned to face them. "Okay . . . where we off to, kids?"

"Mordacity Pride." Jayne checked her comm. "We want to see what she has to say for herself."

"Preferably before my brother kills her."

Jayne gave him a false grin. "Or we get killed."

Hauk tsked. "Now, now. There will be no dying on my watch."

Her smile turned genuine. "One good thing about an Andarion . . ."

"We provide a lot of shade?"

She laughed at Hauk. "No. Loyalty and honor above all."

A dark shadow appeared behind that disconcerting gaze. She glanced to Hadrian who winced.

"There are assholes everywhere, Hauk."

"Stay out of my head, Tris."

"I will try. Sadly, it's not always up to me. I can't help what gets through."

Grimacing, Hauk made a scratching gesture on each side of his face.

Hadrian cringed as he dropped his backpack and covered his eyes with his hands. "Stop it! You're killing me!"

"Yeah, well. You traipse there and you get where my thoughts go."

Hadrian grimaced. "I need brain bleach."

Syn handed him the bottle of Tondarion Fire. "It does wonders."

"Thanks." He took a swig before he turned back to Jayne. "You ready?"

"Lead and I will follow."

Hadrian paused at her flippant words. Though he couldn't read her, they struck him strangely as he had a feeling she didn't really say them lightly.

He handed the whisky back to Syn before he resisted the urge to clap Hauk on the arm again. While he meant what he said about protecting them, the Andarion male was still skittish.

Not that he blamed him. Hauk had his own demons.

Maybe I was lucky, after all.

With his family dead, there had been no one to stab him through his heart. Poor Hauk didn't have that. His family had let him down every way imaginable.

It was why Hauk had moved on and made his family with Nykyrian and Syn.

Nykyrian . . .

He had no idea who that was, but from the level of love and loyalty that Syn and Hauk had for him . . . he must be worth it. That was the kind of friendship he'd always wanted.

Someone who had his back. No matter what.

Family isn't just those who share your blood. It's the ones who are willing to bleed for you.

The *Book of Harmony* was very explicit when it came to defining family.

Those who stay. The ones who run toward you in a crisis without an excuse and expect nothing in return.

Who are you kidding, Hadrian?

He didn't believe in their gods. How could he? Honestly, he wasn't even sure why he kept that tattered worn out copy of the *Harmony* that Nero had given him when he'd been a boy.

The only explanation he had was sentimentality. It'd belonged to their father who had given it to Nero when he'd gone through confirmation.

But unlike his brother, Hadrian didn't think for one moment that some esoteric god gave a single shit about them. If He had, He would have stopped the annihilation of a peaceful race before it happened.

Still . . .

He liked the poetry of the book. The optimism. Even if it was pithy bullshit at times.

You have to believe in something, kiddo.

He could hear Nero's voice in his head. Along with his automatic response. "I believe in me."

Maybe that was all there was to life. Believing in yourself. Because everyone else would just disappoint and hurt you.

When all was said and done, you came into the world alone and you left it that way.

By yourself.

But deep in a place where he wanted to deny it existed was a bitter yearning for something more.

For someone.

I'm a fucking idiot.

He'd go with that. Especially as he watched the way Jayne moved. The confidence and swagger.

She was exceptional.

Right in front of him. Everything he could ask for and more.

Yet he was bound to die old and alone because reaching out just wasn't in the cards. At least not for the likes of him.

Life sucked. Always had and always would. That was the problem when you didn't dare expose yourself. Be yourself. Because deep inside there was no way for anyone to accept you and you knew it.

And still that yearning remained. Damn Jayne for reawakening what he'd finally managed to bury. This was cruel and it was torture.

Yet as they reached the landing bay, his thoughts stopped abruptly.

Hauk slowed as Jayne pulled back.

"Anyone else see what I do?"

Jayne nodded slowly in answer to Hauk's question.

Hadrian immediately homed in on what they saw. Two men dressed in assassin gear were hovering around his ship.

Hauk grinned at her. "Blasting our way out?"

Shaking his head, Hadrian cast his gaze toward a third assassin. "Not the place or the time."

"What do you propose we do?" Jayne looked around at their possible exits.

Hadrian smiled. "Hauk? Put your comm in."

"And?"

"Walk through there as if you're speaking to someone. Tell them an assassin hit your target in the *Devil's Vein* and you're going home, empty-handed."

Hauk scowled. "Why?"

"Decoy them." Now Jayne was smiling. "I like it."

"What if it doesn't work?"

"We fight." Hadrian pulled his backpack off his shoulders. "Let's try the easier path first, shall we?"

Hauk snorted. "Did that once. Still have the scars from that stupidity." He scratched his eye and sighed. "Fine. It's a good day to die." Tapping his ear, he headed toward Hadrian's ship. "Yeah . . . was a total waste of time. Target was already taken. He's dead."

Jayne watched as the assassins frowned at Hauk.

And didn't move.

She cursed their luck. "It's not working."

Hadrian cocked his head. "They're not looking for me." His eyes turned a lighter shade. "They're hunting *you*."

Those words shocked her. "Me?"

He nodded slowly.

And an instant later, someone opened fire on them.

Drawing her blaster, she ducked and slid behind the nearest ship with Hadrian one step behind her. "At least you're big enough to make a great shield."

He made a loud, undignified sound as he pulled his own weapon. "How did they find us?"

"That's a question only a Trisani can answer."

Hadrian didn't really appreciate her glibness. Even if it was true. "Get to the ship and I'll cover you."

She fired two shots. "One problem . . . Your ship. Your biolock."

The engines turned on.

Jayne turned to face him with a gape.

"It'll open for you."

She sputtered before snapping her jaw shut and nodding. Without another word, she ran.

Hadrian used his powers and his blaster to make sure she made it.

She climbed up his ship.

Just as he started running, a blast of color flashed past him, toward the assassins.

It was Hauk. "Got your six."

Yes, he did. Hadrian dodged the next ship and ran for everything he wasn't worth toward his own.

Jayne laid down cover fire as he quickly ran through the bay. He rushed up the ladder and was almost inside when a blast shot hit his leg.

Sucking his breath in sharply, he slipped and almost fell from the ladder.

To his amazement, Jayne caught him and helped him regain his footing.

He looked up and froze as he saw the last thing he'd ever expected. Real concern.

She actually cared that he'd been hurt.

"C'mon, Hadrian. You gotta help me, son. You weigh a lot. I can't pick you up and put you in your seat."

Laughing in spite of the pain, he slid into the cockpit and lowered the canopy.

"Hauk?"

"Yeah. We're in, but Hadrian was hit."

"How bad?" Hauk asked.

She peered around the seat. "Looks pretty foul."

"I'm okay."

"He really doesn't look okay."

Hauk fired his engines. "Can you tend it?"

Hadrian scowled as he ran through his settings. "I'm good enough to get us out of here. I'll be fine. Trust me."

Jayne was thrown back into her seat as he launched them. "You going to pass out again?"

"Hope not."

She peered over the seat as they broke through the atmosphere. "Shouldn't I be the one driving?"

By the tic in his jaw, she knew he was in too much pain to banter.

His breathing was starting to become labored.

"You okay?"

Hadrian nodded as he set the autopilot. With a vicious hiss, he began to unbuckle his pants.

"Um, hey . . . what are you doing?"

"Exposing my wound."

Yeah, that wasn't all that was getting exposed. Jayne sat back in her seat as she tried not to think about how endowed her companion was.

But those thoughts died as she saw a low light emanating in front of her.

Scowling, she leaned forward again to see him running his hand over the fierce injury. Damn. He was lucky he'd made into the cockpit with *that*.

It was a vicious, bloody burn that had to be killing him.

Just as she was about to climb over the seat and help, he let go of his leg.

Her jaw dropped.

It was healed.

"Did you do that?"

With a long sigh, he leaned back and nodded.

"You okay?"

"I will be." Hadrian wiped at the sweat on his forehead. "For some reason, healing doesn't drain me as much as using my powers for other things."

"Really?"

"Yeah. Nero says that we all have something we can do without paying a price for it. Mine seems to be healing."

She wished she had that ability. "That's a good one to have."

He didn't speak as he pulled his pants back on.

"Hey, humans? You still with me?"

Hadrian opened the channel. "We're here, Hauk. Is that you on my tail?"

"It is. I'm waiting on you to send me the nav I need for where we're headed."

Hadrian entered the sequence in and then sent it over to Hauk.

"Thanks. By the way, do we need to stop and get help for you?"

"No. I healed it."

"Can you confirm that, Jayne?"

She smiled at the doubt in Hauk's tone. "Yeah. He's perfect." Especially that tight eight pack she'd seen when he undid his pants.

"Noted. A Tris and an Andarion make an awesome team."

"What about me?" She was actually offended.

Until Hauk responded. "Aren't you Andarion?"

Oh ... "I guess I am."

"Then, there you are."

She was amazed at how much she liked their Andarion bodyguard. He was very charming in his own unique way. Like Hadrian who was too charming, if the truth was told.

Don't go there...

But it was hard after the half-naked image of him was seared into her mind.

Luckily, her link chose that moment to go crazy and distract her from dangerous contemplations.

Hadrian looked back at her. "What's that?"

She pulled it out.

A horrible feeling washed over her as she read the content. Of course, it didn't help that there was a giant picture of her along with a bounty that made Hadrian's paltry. "What the hell?"

"No idea," Hadrian said from in front of her. "I don't know what you're looking at."

Grimacing, she handed her link to Hadrian whose eyes widened as he read it. "Sorry."

"You should be, punk'n. You got me killed."

Hadrian tsked at her. "You're not dead yet."

"With a bounty that high, my prospects for survival aren't very likely."

"But you forgot your secret weapon."

A Trisani. She should be flattered and yet ...

"Yeah. I'm glad Hauk is with us."

"Pardon?"

Laughing at his offense in spite of her concern, she took her link back. But no sooner did she get it than it went off with a unique sound.

"What's that?" Hadrian asked.

She placed her finger on it so that she could answer. "Normally means I finished my mission." She answered it quickly because if she failed to answer it, it could cause an interstellar incident. "Hey, sis." Jayne adjusted herself in her seat. "No . . . still alive in spite of the notice you just received that said I'm dead. Amazing, right?"

Hadrian shook his head as he realized what had happened. That they'd been declared dead. "Syn intervention?"

She nodded to let him know he'd guessed correctly. "Yeah. Love you, too, Evie. Talk soon."

Hadrian let out a long-suffering sigh. "Couldn't he have done that sooner?"

"Knowing Syn and his fear of your brother and my sister, I'm pretty sure he did it as fast as he could."

"You're probably right."

Jayne saw him cringe as his own link went off. "Nero?"

"Who else? Guess Mama N wants to change my diaper and burp me." As he answered, she could just imagine the smirk on his adorable face. "Still alive, my brother. You?"

"You're not funny."

Jayne pressed her lips together at Nero's furious tone that was so loud, she could hear it plainly over the ship's engines.

"I'm hilarious," Hadrian said without pausing. "You just have no appreciation for my humor."

"Not when I'm getting a notification that you've been terminated. How the hell could I find *that* funny?"

Yeah, she could understand why Nero was a little hot.

"I can see where that might wreck your day. Especially mine if I died."

"Don't make me kick your ass, Hady."

Hadrian grinned at Jayne. "Have to find me first."

Before Nero responded, he cut the transmission. "And when he does, he's going to kill me."

She wiggled her comm. "Mine, too." She tucked it away, then jerked her chin toward his ship. "So, where are we headed?"

"What was your expression? Hell in a handbasket?"

"Now I understand your urge to head-slap me. Can I get a better response?"

He piped the nav coordinates so that she could see them over his head. "We're going to the last known location for Mordacity. There, we will interrogate and probably kill her . . . provided Nero doesn't get there first and beat us to the execution."

Chapter Five

J ayne looked around the harsh metal space station that was owned by the Septurnum group of the Tavali pirate nation. There were enough ships here that it looked like a League port. Every crew functioned with military precision and her group was being eyed as if they were a lethal STD in a brothel. "What kind of assassin lives in a Tavali station?"

Hadrian laughed. "A smart one."

She scowled. "How so?"

"League laws don't apply here. Even though the League refuses to recognize the Tavali as a legitimate empire, they are still a sovereign nation."

Jayne conceded that point. They were also a massive one that was divided into four separate states with the Septurnums being the group that was held out as a rebel band from the other three Tavali nations. Even among their own, the Tavalis didn't trust the Septs.

And because the Tavali's existence wasn't recognized by the League, they were all considered outlaws. Anyone found with Tavali gear or flags could be imprisoned or executed. The only thing that kept most empires from declaring war on them was that no one knew exactly how many Tavali there actually were.

Or how much fire power their nation had access to. Since they were literally pirates who made their homes on space stations spread out through the Ichidian universe, no one wanted to risk going to war with them.

Only the League was that stupid.

Because the main rule of the Tavali was a simple one . . . they were one united family. If you messed with one of them, they were all honor bound to retaliate.

That had been the foundation of their empire. A solo shipper and her crew who'd been wrongfully persecuted by the Krellins who had them all executed. The parents of that captain, Tavali Snitch, had rallied all the independent shippers they could, and created a nation other empires would be afraid to prey on.

For that reason, most nations wisely turned a blind eye to Tavali activities and allowed them to go their own way so long as they didn't cause any insurrections or other problems that the recognized leaders had to deal with.

Don't start no shit, won't be no shit. That should have been the Tavali national motto instead of *Hem me never.*

Which got back to her original question. "Given how territorial and exclusive the Tavali are, why would they ever allow an outsider to reside in one of their bases?"

Hadrian glanced at Hauk as he joined them before he answered her. "I'm going to hazard a guess that she's not an outsider."

Jayne scowled at that. "Tavali aren't assassins."

"Technically, Tavali don't exist as they're made up of all species of sentient beings. So, why couldn't someone be both?"

Hauk nodded. "That tracks."

Jayne wasn't so sure. "I just can't see a pirate as a licensed assassin."

Hadrian put the heel of his hand against his temple as they stepped away from their ship. "There's a lot of anger in the Tavali, isn't there?"

"You okay?"

He shook his head and winced. "Not sure. But if I go down, we now have help." He gestured at Hauk.

"Really? Why do I always get stuck carrying the idiot?"

Hadrian started to clap his arm again, then caught himself. "Your awesome Andarion strength."

Hauk snorted. "Wishing I was Tavali at the moment."

Those words had barely left his lips before a tall man wearing a black battlesuit trimmed in red approached them like a wary predator. "Can I help you?" His gaze went from Hauk to Hadrian and finally to her.

Little did he know, she was probably the more lethal of this bunch, given the fury that forever gripped her.

Hadrian jumped in before either of them could speak. "I'm here to see Mordacity Pride."

The man's eyes narrowed, especially as he noted the blood on Hadrian's pants. "Why?"

Hadrian turned charming. "Don't worry about *that*. I cut my leg climbing into my ship." He turned around to show it to the Tavali. "Nothing nefarious. As for Mordacity, she's a friend of my brother's and by friend, I mean intimate. I wanted to thank her for saving his life."

That didn't seem to allay the man's fears at all. "Who's your brother?"

"Rather not say, Relic. But I know you from the stories she's told my brother. How's your wife doing? Is Vatrice flying again?"

He put his hand on his blaster and stepped back as if he was about to draw it. "Anyone could find that out."

"But would they know about that little escapade you and Mordacity had two weeks ago?"

The man's eyes flared as he glanced around the base. "Lower your voice!"

"Sorry," Hadrian whispered. "Wasn't trying to get you into trouble. I just need to know where Section H-16 housing is so that I can personally thank her."

The Tavali turned slightly. "Down that hallway until you hit the center atrium. Veer left and you'll be right there."

Hadrian clapped him on the shoulder. "Thanks."

Jayne quickened her steps as Hadrian took off in that direction.

Once she was sure the Tavali wasn't following them, she tapped his shoulder, then jerked her chin toward the Tavali. "What was all that?"

"People telegraph all manner of things when they're confronting someone. You'd be amazed at the thoughts in their heads."

"Only thing I think about is killing them," Hauk said.

Hadrian laughed at Hauk's comment. "Mostly, you think about what your brother, Fain, would do."

"Get out of my head."

"I really wish it was that easy. Sadly, I don't want to be there anymore than you want me traipsing through your emotional baggage." Hadrian stopped and turned to Jayne. "Thank you for being silent."

"Not sure I have anything to do with that, but you're welcome."

The look on Hadrian's face was so sincere that it tightened her throat.

Before she realized what he was doing, he leaned his forehead against hers and closed his eyes.

Unsure of how to respond, she arched a brow. "You okay?"

Instead of speaking, Hadrian lifted her hands and put them on each side of his head.

She cut a sideways glance to Hauk who had the same confusion on his face that she felt.

Hadrian let out a long sigh. "I wish I could walk around like this."

"Why?"

"Whatever it is in you, it blocks it all out. No idea why, but the silence is heaven." He brushed her hands through his hair before he straightened up. "Sorry. I just needed a little break."

Not sure how to feel, she smiled at him. "No problem. You better now?"

"Think so. But I'm wondering how my brother can function among so many other people. Most days, I want to scream out until they commit me."

"Well, my hands are at your service whenever you need them." Jayne regretted that sentence the moment she said it out loud.

Especially as Hauk laughed and Hadrian gaped.

"Not what I meant! Oh my God! Really?"

Now Hadrian was laughing. "All good, *suāva*."

That word gave her pause. *"Suāva?"*

He actually blushed. "It's an endearment."

"Which means?"

"I'm afraid if I tell you, you might kick me in the balls."

She wasn't sure what her expression was, but it caused Hadrian to quickly step behind Hauk.

"How do you stand not knowing what other people are thinking?" Hadrian asked Hauk.

Hauk shrugged nonchalantly. "Apparently, you have a good idea to be doing that kind of tap dance around me."

Jayne leaned over to peer around Hauk's massive

form to where Hadrian was hiding. "Just what did you call me?"

Hadrian's cheeks reddened even more. "Sweetie."

Now, she was even more confused by his actions. "Why would I assault you for that?"

"I just remember my brother telling me that women don't like it and not to use it unless I was really familiar with the woman or wanted to get kicked in my balls."

Jayne rubbed at her forehead. "Well, I can't speak for how often Nero gets a kick to his jewels, but you're safe from me . . . at least for the moment."

"Joyous."

Hauk shook his head at them. "Don't we have something more productive and dangerous we should be doing?"

"Yes, we do." Hadrian finally stepped around him to lead them toward this mysterious Tavali assassin.

Jayne wasn't sure exactly who they'd be meeting. Given the legends of the Trisani, she expected someone regal and refined.

Or raw and lethal.

But when Hadrian knocked on the door and it opened to reveal Mordacity, she was a little stunned.

Not only did she have the bearing of a Ring prize fighter, but she wore smudged, heavy black eye makeup around her eyes that were so dark, it blended with her eye color. Indeed, that makeup made it hard to see if she had her eyes opened or closed.

Her black hair was pulled back from her angular face. Her *green* angular face that held a bold black geometric pattern. Jayne wasn't sure if that pattern was a tattoo, or natural.

But it wasn't just those factors that caught her off guard. Mordacity was absolutely tiny. As in she barely reached the middle of Jayne's chest. Never mind the two males who towered over her like trees.

And it wasn't just her height. She was so skinny that she reminded Jayne of a street beggar.

How could this tiny little waif be an assassin?

Mordacity scowled at their group. "Can I help you?"

Hadrian heard the question, but he was too fascinated by the frail sprig of a woman in front of him. To save his life, he couldn't imagine his brother with someone like her.

Nero usually preferred robust, tall women.

In fact, he couldn't figure out how Nero didn't crush her. She was more the size of a doll than a full-grown woman.

And as she swept a gaze over him, she took a step back . . .

"Yeah," he said as her thoughts hit him. "I'm actually taller than Nero. But don't feel bad, you're not what I expected either."

Mordacity's gaze narrowed. "Why are you here?"

When Jayne started forward, Hadrian gently took her arm to stop her.

"She's innocent."

Jayne scowled at him. "Wait. What?"

"She really has no idea why I'm here."

"Stop playing in my head!" Mordacity growled at him. "Can't stand it when Nero does it and I don't want you there, either."

He held his hands up in surrender. "You know I can't help it. But can we come in for a minute?"

She glanced to Hauk as if debating. Finally, she stepped back so that they could enter her teeny apartment.

Hadrian walked to the small living room that wasn't

made to host a large group. Hauk, alone, took up most of it.

Mordacity shut the door, then turned to face them. "So . . . ?"

There was no easy way to break it to her. "Jayne? Can you show her what Syn gave us?"

"Sure." Jayne turned it on and handed it over.

As soon as Mordacity saw the warrant and information Syn had traced that pegged her as the culprit, she paled. "Is this a joke?"

"That's what *we're* wondering."

"I had nothing to do with this. How stupid would I have to be?"

Mordacity had a point. Only an idiot would go against his brother, especially given their ability to pick the truth out of her head.

Jayne took her link back. "You think someone's setting you both up?"

Maybe. Hadrian could see that. It would make sense. "How close are you to Nero?"

She held her hands up and made a hilarious face. "Your brother doesn't share his feelings. I'm sure you know this. Some days, he's like talking to a wall."

Hadrian shook his head. "I wouldn't say that given he tends to express himself quite freely around me. And more often than I like."

"Lucky you. He's a silent grave to me. I can barely get a meal preference out of him, and most of our conversations are me talking and him grunting." She looked at Jayne. "Can I see that again?"

"Sure." Jayne returnedthe link to her.

Her frown deepened. "Why didn't this come up on my bounty sheets?"

Hadrian had no answer for that. "Jayne?"

"It should have, if she's licensed."

"I'm licensed." Mordacity picked up her own link, then handed it over to Jayne. "How is this possible?"

Jayne gaped as she saw the truth, then passed it to Hadrian. "She's blocked from it."

"That makes no sense."

Jayne agreed. She met Mordacity's confused stare. "How shielded is this place?"

"Meaning?"

"If I call someone in the League, will they be able to pinpoint my location."

Mordacity laughed. "No. If they try, it'll ping them all over the universe. We don't take those chances."

Hauk narrowed his gaze. "So, you *are* Tavali."

She nodded.

"Born and raised?"

"No," Hadrian answered for her. "She was born Phrixian."

Jayne's jaw dropped even more at that disclosure. "I've never met a Phrixian before."

"Lucky you. Keep praying that I'm your lifetime limit."

Wow. Even Jayne caught the bitterness in those words. "You ran away?"

"Yeah. And if my people find me, they'll kill me."

"Why?"

"I'm Schvardan and I'm AWOL from our military. No one in our service goes AWOL. It's treason. Any Schvardan who sees me is honor bound to kill me. And a Naglfari would just kill me for fun."

Jayne was baffled. "Then why would you did you leave the military?"

"Because I had to protect my family. No matter what it cost me personally."

"I can see why my brother likes you."

She didn't respond to Hadrian's comment. "Who would have the ability to do this?"

Jayne shrugged. "No idea, but could you help us out by repealing the warrant?"

Mordacity blinked fast and stepped back at Jayne's question. "Of course! Oh my God, I'm so sorry. I was so focused on me that I didn't even think about what this had done to the two of you." She pulled out her link and typed in her code.

Jayne smiled at Hadrian and Hauk as relief poured over her.

Sadly, it wasn't long-lived.

By Mordacity's expression, she could tell there was a massive problem.

"What?"

Mordacity's frown deepened. "I can't cancel it."

Jayne felt sick to her stomach. "What?"

Mordacity stepped closer to show her. "Correct me if I'm wrong, but shouldn't I have the ability to close this down?"

Jayne took her comm and looked at the screen. There was a spot to withdraw the contract, but when she pressed it, nothing happened. "This isn't good."

Stunned, she handed it off to Hadrian. He cursed as he attempted the same thing she had.

And failed just as miserably.

Hauk cleared his throat and held his hand out. "Since we're all participating in a futile exercise, may I?"

"Sure." Hadrian gave it to him, then looked to Jayne. "If this is like a jar of jam, and that bastard gets it to work, I'll scream."

She burst out laughing at his unexpected comment.

Hauk snorted and handed the comm back to Mordacity. "No need in straining our hearing. Damn thing's busted."

"All right. That's it." She dialed for Jinx who answered so fast that it made her jump.

"Where the hell are you?"

"Good to hear from you, too."

"Don't play this shit, Jayne. I have your sister climbing a wall and threatening body parts I'd like to keep. You have completely vanished off every bit of tracking software and hardware I have. If Syn's the one who gave it to you, I'm going for *his* balls."

"Syn had nothing to do with it." Not entirely true. since he'd been the one to come up with the address, but . . . "So, let's keep everyone anatomically correct, okay?"

"Jayne–"

"I'm fine, Jinx. Really, but I have a weird question for you."

"Of course, you do. What is it?"

"Remember when you told me that I could have the warrant withdrawn?"

"I remember telling you it would be next to impossible."

"Yeah well, I'm standing here with the woman who took it out . . . supposedly, but it won't let her withdraw it."

Jinx went silent for a second. "What?"

Jayne handed her link to Mordacity. "Tell him."

"Hi whoever this is. According to the paperwork, I'm the one who did it, but I didn't do it. It shows up on my link that I could, in theory, release the contract. But the button isn't working."

"You had nothing to do with this?"

"No." Mordacity swallowed hard. "I have nothing against Hadrian, and I don't know Jayne. And I'm definitely not dumb enough to take out a contract on someone who has a brother who would beat me senseless and leave me dead for it."

"So, Hedlund, what's your bright idea now?" Jayne asked.

Jinx really didn't appreciate her sarcastic use of the famous scientist. "I think you need to tell me where you are."

"Not until we figure this out."

"Jayne . . . stop a minute and think this through. Who would have the ability to do what you're telling me?"

"C.I. Syn?"

Hadrian rolled his eyes while Hauk snorted.

Jinx cleared his throat impatiently. "A techspert wouldn't have the clearance."

That made her stomach shrink. "What are you saying?"

"Think, Jaynie. Whoever framed Mordacity has to be a League member or have a really strong connection."

Hauk nodded. "He's right. You'd have to be on their servers and system to deactivate that button on a contract."

Now they were all baffled. "Who in the League would have something against us?"

"Did I just hear Hauk with you?" Jinx asked.

Why was she even surprised? "How do you know Hauk?"

"We have a mutual friend."

"I'm here, Shadowborne. What do you need?"

"Feel better knowing you're with them. Can you please keep them from doing something stupid?"

"I doubt it, but I can try."

"Good . . . I'm going to pull my team together and look into this. Stay out of trouble and keep your heads low while I contact them. Can you do that?"

Jayne growled at Jinx's request. "We need to know who's after us and why."

"I know, but you can't access League files and you

know it. You'll get killed the moment you access them. Stay put and try to find some patience."

As much as she hated to admit it, he was right. "Fine. Don't take too long."

* * *

Jinx cut the transmission and cursed at his luck. He needed to contact his League compadres, but if he didn't call and let Eve know that her sister was all right, she might make good her threat to castrate him.

He punched in her frequency and waited.

"Did you find her?"

The fact that Eve didn't even ask about him told him how worried she was. She was always terrified of losing him. "Not exactly."

"What does that mean?"

He really wanted to tell her to calm down, but his past experience with that stupidity caused him to bite his tongue. "I just spoke to her."

"Where is she?"

"Living on Outpost Jayne, as usual. Not listening to any reason . . . which I take is an Erixour specialty?"

"Don't, Jinx. Not in the mood."

"I know, baby. Just trying to lighten your stress."

"Then get my sister back here so that I can kick her scrawny ass."

"Working on it. She's safe for the moment and I need to make some calls before she runs through her tiny patience and does something profoundly stupid to make us both crazy."

She sighed. "Fine. You be careful."

"You, too." He ended the call, then pressed the digits for his safety valve. The one person besides Eve that he knew he could trust with anything.

Which was insane really, given that Savage was one of the most ruthless assassins the League had ever trained.

None of them were ever supposed to care about anyone else. Kill or be killed.

Yet Savage answered immediately. "Problem?"

He smiled at his friend's opening question. Not that he blamed him.

While Jinx ran with a small handful of League assassin rebels, Savage was their leader and they rarely contacted him unless it was an emergency.

"Always."

Savage snorted. "Who do I have to kill?"

"That remains to be seen. But right now, I have a slight problem. Eve's sister took a contract for retrieval and once she was signed on, it was switched to a kill warrant."

"Yeah . . . and?"

"She found the person that our system says took it out, but there's no way to rescind it and she claims she didn't take it out."

Savage didn't respond.

"Did you hear me?"

"I heard. Just ruminating over an impossibility. What do you mean, it can't be rescinded?"

"I'm sending it to you now. As you can see, someone tapped our system and removed the ability to cancel the warrant."

Savage took a moment before he spoke again. "What fucked up shit is this?"

"I was hoping you'd have some idea. Ever seen anything like it before?"

"No. There's always a cancel code."

But not this time. "Are you thinking what I'm thinking?"

Savage sent the warrant back to him. "That it's one of our assassins or high commanders? Yeah."

"It would have to be, right?"

"Yes, it would. I don't care how good a techspert is, if they went near our system, Quiakides would have them gutted within an hour."

Yeah, their prime commander didn't play. He was a nasty bastard, which was why his son, Nykyrian, was counted among their small group of rebels. Nyk had one rule– if anyone other than him killed his father, their prime commander, he'd gut them.

Apparently, there were some serious childhood issues stemming from the Quiakides' home.

And that made him miss his own family. The only issue Jinx had was with his was his uncle who'd slaughtered his parents and sold him to the League.

If it was the last thing he did, he was going to kill that sick sonofabitch.

But that would have to wait. Right now, he had to take care of Jayne.

Savage spoke again, breaking him out of his moping. "Whoever did this was sewing massive strife between Scalera and Pride."

"Yeah, I had the same thought. But who in the League would give a shit about either one?"

"You'll have to interview them. Find out who has a connection."

Jinx sighed. "I'm the only one I know who has a connection."

"Excuse me?"

"I'm related to the Scaleras through my maternal grandmother. She was the only sister to Nero's father."

"Are you fucking kidding me?"

"No." But sadly, he had no Trisani abilities other than a heightened sense of awareness and some very minimal precog. "But no one knows that. It's not even in my records."

"Are you sure no one knows it? They could be targeting you again."

"But why? It's not like I've ever had much if any contact with them. I wouldn't know Nero if I passed him on the street. And I can't imagine any of them deliberately going near the League given what happened to their homeworld. As far as I know, any surviving Scaleras scattered to the wind and have kept all their collective heads low so as not to lose them."

"Then focus on Pride. Does she have any League contacts?"

"I'll find out."

"Let me know if I can help."

"Thanks, Sav."

"Thank me by surviving. Don't lose your head over this."

"Will do, Commander."

Snorting, Sav cut the transmission.

Jinx sat in his ship, thinking about everything he'd learned.

Mordacity Pride.

There was next to no information in their system about her. Which meant it was an alias. Had to be.

Even though they were damn near impossible to pull off with the League, there were a handful of people, such as Syn, who had managed to create new identities in their databases and get away with it.

Who had helped Mordacity?

And why? What was she hiding? That was the real question.

Chapter Six

"I don't like this." Jayne paced the room in front of Hadrian.

"Totally off topic, but I envy you for being able to do that."

"Do what?"

"Walk and not bump into anything."

Laughing, she shook her head. It was true. He was so large that he took up most of the couch and had chosen to sit so that he wouldn't accidentally bump into anything.

"You are cute, though."

"Cute?" He arched a brow at her. "Not adorably sexy?"

"Is that what you want?"

He rubbed at his forehead. "What I want is to be with Hauk and Mordacity. I hate being trapped in here."

"I didn't realize I was that obnoxious."

He shook his head. "It's not you. You have to remember that I've been in hiding my entire life." Hadrian gestured at the room. "This . . . makes me crazy. All I want is my freedom. To be like someone normal who can walk around without looking over my shoulder all the time."

"I get it. I hate being an assassin. More than you can imagine. This was not what I saw for my life."

"Yeah. I wanted to own my own store. I always thought how much fun it would be to welcome customers and interact with them without fear."

Jayne sat down on the coffee table in front of him. "I wanted to be a teacher."

"Really?"

She nodded slowly. "I wanted to be surrounded by kids."

He actually gaped at her.

"Don't act so surprised. Why are you surprised?"

"Just . . ." He indicated her with both his hands. "You're amazing at what you do. I can't see you not kicking ass and taking names."

With a heavy sigh, she rested her elbows on her thighs and leaned down. "Again, not what I wanted to be. Just once, I'd like to wear heels. To dress without worrying if my concealed weapons are showing." Jayne scowled as he started smiling. "You find that funny?"

He sobered instantly. "Not at all. But it dawned on me how refreshing it is to sit here and not know what your thoughts are. This is what it's like for normal people to converse . . . I never had a clue before."

"I can't imagine being lambasted by everyone's thoughts all the time."

"The only helpful part is knowing when someone's about to take a shot at my head. And that's the most disconcerting part about being with you. I never realized before how much I depend on the abilities I've always said I hated."

Jayne reached out and touched his knee. "So, you really have no idea what I'm thinking?"

"Not even a little."

Impishly, she sprang forward and tickled him.

Hadrian had no idea what to expect and it shocked him that his arms were suddenly full of Jayne. No one had ever really played with him. Not even when he was a kid.

Laughing, he grabbed her hands. "Stop! I yield!"

She did but kept her hands on his abdomen. There was a glint in her eyes that he didn't understand.

Not until she leaned forward and kissed him.

The soft touch of her lips on his . . .

It set fire to his blood. Closing his eyes, he surrendered himself to her affection.

Jayne smiled as she breathed in the scent of cinnamon and spice. Hadrian had an infectious scent that made him taste all the sweeter.

What had begun as a prank was no longer feeling that way. Especially given the fact that he held her so tenderly that it melted her will to withdraw.

You need to stop!

The voice in her head roared, but she couldn't help herself. It'd been too long since she'd found anyone she'd been interested in. Too long since she'd allowed herself to be attracted to someone.

He was everything she'd wanted.

And everything she couldn't have.

She knew it. What he wanted and what she prayed for were completely different goals.

The only thing they had in common was that they were both wanted dead.

And she was supposed to kill him.

No, she was *required* to kill him.

Thank the gods that he couldn't hear her thoughts, or he'd probably strangle her.

Still . . .

She couldn't say no. Not right now.

Not like this.

Hadrian growled as she deepened their kiss. He couldn't get enough of her.

Not after this raw, sensual taste and the newfound addiction to her buried him in a landslide.

With every breath, he wanted her more. Wanted to wear her scent on his skin.

Every beat of his heart was a reminder of how she made it race. How much he was grateful that she'd careened into his precarious life and set it on fire.

Even if she'd been sent there to abduct and then kill him.

I'm so fucked up.

But at least he knew it. And now that he held her . .

.

Impatience grabbed hold of him.

They didn't have time. Any moment, Hauk and Mordacity could return.

Still, he couldn't withdraw from her. It'd been too long since he'd last been with anyone.

Way too long, now that he thought about it. But what choice did he have? He couldn't afford to let anyone in to his screwed up life.

And yet Jayne had crawled inside him far deeper than anyone else. Maybe it was because she was silent to him.

With her, it was all discovery. Exploration.

The taste of her that lingered on his tongue.

Jayne pulled back, her gaze fixed on him as if nothing else existed. Before he could think or move, she nestled against his chest. Her arms wrapped around his ribs and a tightness he hadn't noticed eased with her touch.

Her breasts pressed against him, and her hands fell

way too close to the part of him that ached to merge with her.

Damn it . . .

How could he be this hungry for a woman who was supposed to end him?

Hell, at the rate they were going, he might die for want of her.

Her one hand dipped lower still and wrung a moan from deep within his soul.

"That's what I want to hear." She breathed against his ear.

In that moment, Hadrian felt his control slipping. "Jayne . . . you've no idea what you're unleashing."

"You won't hurt me."

She had no idea. One of the reasons he'd avoided sex as much as he could was what happened when Trisani were intimate. "It's not that."

Jayne gasped as she felt an unbelievable surge against her entire body. It was electric . . . like a thousand different tongues all over her. But more than that, she could feel Hadrian inside her even though they were both completely dressed.

Her heart hammering, she came instantly.

When she met Hadrian's gaze, she saw that odd shade of blue that meant his powers were active.

"What just happened?"

"That is why my people are enslaved when they find us."

"Can you feel it?"

"Normally, but not with you. I can only see the pleasure on your face."

Holy shit . . .

He started to pull away.

Jayne stopped him. "Where are you going?"

"Figured you were done with me."

She shook her head slowly. "Are you kidding?" Slowly, she slid from his lap and took his hand.

Don't do this...

But it was too late. There was no way she could stop now.

Not to mention the fact that she didn't want to. So, she led him to the small bedroom.

Hadrian was completely stunned by her actions. More stunned that he'd lost control with her. *Gauduley.* That was the Trisani term for when one was so attracted to another that they lost control of their powers.

It could be dangerous. An unfettered Tris could accidentally reach out. It was why his race had always prided itself on utmost control. Why they couldn't afford to let down their guard.

And it didn't happen with every encounter.

There had to be the *incelebratus*– that special connection with the other party. No one knew what caused it. How it formed or why.

It simply was and came without warning.

But he understood it, at least in part. Jayne fit him in so many ways. She was patience when he wanted to rush, calm when he raged.

And she soothed him when nothing else did.

That alone could bring him to his knees.

Claiming her lips again, he smiled as she lifted to her toes. Then his full attention was on her taste. Their tongues danced, a sensual tango.

He needed more. Needed all of her.

"The door is open." He pressed his lips to hers.

She pulled back with a laugh. "Think Mordacity will kill us?"

"Probably. But what the hell? She was the one who took the hit out on me."

Jayne laughed again. "So *you* say."

"Either way, she owes us."

Releasing him, Jayne led the way into the bedroom.

The sway of her hips was a private invitation. His breathing ragged, he shut the door with the heel of his hand and locked the world from their haven.

The buzz of the well-tended lock satisfied him. Before he could turn around, her hands slid under the edge of his jacket. They were so warm that her touch set fire to him.

His forehead hit the door and he froze to savor her touch. Chills ran across his chest. His nipples drew into tight buds. The breath he'd thought to release locked in his lungs.

All his blood fled south, and his thoughts tangled between his need to stop her and his desire to make sure she didn't.

Her hands traveled his spine before reaching around to the front. Deft fingers made short work of his shirt, then slid down lower. She caressed him through his pants.

He trembled at the fire that rushed the length of his body. God help him. He'd never felt like this before.

Never been touched by a woman whose thoughts weren't overriding his.

Grasping her hands, he pulled them away from him. "If you don't stop, we'll both be disappointed."

She snorted at those words. "I've already had my fun, punk'n."

Her humor was infectious. "In that case . . ." Hadrian released her hands long enough to sweep her into his arms.

He carried her to the bed, then lowered her toward the mattress.

"Thank you for not groaning when you picked me up."

"What?"

She nuzzled his cheek. "Nothing kills a woman's desire faster than the sound of her lover groaning from her weight. You made me feel weightless. Thank you."

He laughed until her body slid along his, every inch inciting a fire he wanted to bathe inside.

A fire that was stoked when Jayne began to slowly undo her clothes. Dumbfounded and overwhelmed, he couldn't do anything other than watch.

Damn . . .

She was the sexiest thing he'd ever seen.

And she seemed to enjoy him watching her.

Unlike her, he didn't want to waste time. Using his powers, he disrobed immediately.

Grinning, Jayne nodded. "Nice."

"Naughty," he contradicted as he lifted one leg to the bed and almost knocked her over.

She steadied herself as he brought himself up against her.

Unable to believe her beauty, he cupped her ass and brought her to his mouth.

The first taste was all woman. The salty aftertaste was the rarest flavor. He glanced up to see her eyes closed, one hand on her breast and the other clutched in his hair.

Sensing her rising desire, he laid her back on the bed. Her nails scraped his scalp and drove a long shudder along her spine.

Jayne closed her eyes as she again felt that surging throughout her entire body. "How can you do that?"

He smiled down at her. "Another gift."

Biting her lip, she freed his hair from its band so that it fell over his shoulders. "You are gorgeous."

He'd never really felt that way, but he was willing to

accept it from her. Especially as she writhed beneath him.

Unable to stand it, he parted her thighs.

This time, it was she who cupped *his* ass and pulled him closer. She reached between them until she touched his hard shaft.

Hadrian couldn't breathe as she gently explored him from tip to hilt. His head swam.

Every thought in his head shattered.

Jayne shivered as she felt him again, all over her body. There were no words to describe the sensation.

None.

Unable to take it anymore, she carefully guided him into her body.

They moaned in unison.

Jayne swallowed hard as he lowered his lips to take hers again. Then ever so slowly, he began to move against her hips.

Holy minsid shit . . .

His actions only intensified what she felt.

Hadrian bit his lip. He'd wanted to savor this. To lengthen it for as long as he could.

But there was no way.

To hell with a long ride. He needed to claim her, to mark her as his, and he didn't even know why. Something about her reached out to him.

Made him yearn for things he knew he couldn't have.

A home.

A wife . . .

Children.

What the hell? Those had never been in his plans. Not even on the peripheral.

Yet she reached out to a part of him he'd buried so

long ago that he barely remembered ever having those thoughts.

His head swimming, he quickened his strokes, wanting to drive himself in as deep as he could.

She ran her hands down his spine, raising chills the whole way. Her eyes were as drunk as he felt.

Jayne met him stroke for stroke, making him all the more determined to savor every single moment of this.

Every single inch of her.

And when she lifted her hips to take him in even deeper and began to shudder as another orgasm claimed her, it drove him over the edge.

Throwing his head back, he shouted out. Jayne gripped him fiercely as she cradled him with her entire body.

Never in his life had he felt anything like this.

His body still shuddering, he withdrew and rolled to his side, bringing her with him.

He listened as two hearts thundered together. Her touch gentled on his body.

"Am I dead?"

Hadrian laughed at her question. "I know I am."

"Ah, good. At least we went out with a big bang."

Wrinkling his nose, he pulled her closer. "Why do I find you so amusing?"

"My fierce Andarion genes. They call out to everyone."

"Nah. Think it's more your fiercely attractive ass."

She hit him with a pillow. "You're awful."

"Telling you that you have a positively edible rear is offensive? Sorry. I thought women liked that."

She leaned over him and kissed his nose. "Sometimes we do."

Hadrian tucked her hair behind her ear.

Just as he was about to speak again, he heard the sound of the door opening.

Oh shit, Jayne mouthed.

Hadrian quickly slid out of bed. Using his powers, he put his clothes on and dressed Jayne.

"Nice," she whispered.

Grinning, he quickly put the bed back in order.

"Hey! Where are you guys?"

Jayne cringed at Hauk's question. "Uh–"

"We were resting." Hadrian opened the door and stepped out into the hallway. "We didn't know how long you'd be gone, so I went to lie down, and Jayne came to check on me."

She followed him back to the living room where she saw the suspicion on both their faces. Hoping that she wasn't blushing, she slid past Hadrian. "Did you find out anything?"

"As a matter of fact, I did." Stepping aside, she opened the door. "But it wasn't what we were expecting to find."

Hadrian cursed at the tall, arrogant prick who strode in to glare at him. "You're such an asshole."

Nero tsked. "The correct words are, 'Thank you for saving my life again, brother.'"

"Kiss my ass, Nero."

Jayne gaped at that disclosure, even though she probably should have known. But to be fair, they didn't really favor.

Nero's hair was lighter, and his eyes were much paler and more gray than blue. He was also significantly shorter than Hadrian.

And in her opinion, not quite as handsome.

She was so focused on him, that she missed seeing the corner of a chair and fell forward.

Hadrian caught her up against him. "Careful."

Nero sneered. "Put that down! You don't know where she's been."

"Don't know where you've been either, but you expect me to take you in whenever you turn up. And you're not nearly as cute."

"Not nearly as likely to cut your throat, either. Have you forgotten that?"

"I never forget that, Nero. How could I?"

Jayne wanted to be offended by their bantering, but she just felt bad for Hadrian.

Honestly, she understood Nero's protectiveness as it was just how her own sister would have reacted had the tables been reversed.

Nero let out an exasperated sigh. "Do you have any idea how many people are after you right now?"

"Not really. But I do know how many Jayne has taken out for me."

"Oh." Nero at least had the good grace to look sheepish.

"Yeah. *Oh*. So, are we going to keep arguing like morons on parade or are you ready to be human?"

"Shut your stunted ass!"

Hadrian arched a brow at that. "I'm a full head taller than you."

"And you weigh half as much."

Sadly true. He'd tried everything he could think of to bulk up, but for some reason he just couldn't pack on muscles the way his brother did. Another thing about Nero that seriously chafed his ass.

Genes were a screwed-up thing. According to his brother, Hadrian looked nothing like the rest of their siblings. Nero and Auggie had dark blond hair like their mother while Julia and Trajen had been dark-haired like their father. No one knew where Hadrian's brown hair had come from.

With the exception of Nero, he barely remembered

any of his siblings, or his parents. They were more like vague shadows in his mind. Phantoms that haunted him with glimpses of things he wasn't sure were actual memories or stories Nero had told him about them.

More than anything, he wanted to remember. To have that sense of family that Nero had known.

But his mother had been Righteous Anger and his father was Caution.

Some days, they were Hatred and Pain.

He knew nothing else. The foster parents Nero had left him with had always been afraid of being discovered. After all, they harbored the youngest member of the Trisani royal house and were Trisani themselves.

And their fear had turned out to be valid as both of them had been killed when he was only ten years old.

After that, Nero had begun hiding him out with different people for the next eight years.

Then Nero had moved him around to keep him safe.

Hadrian glanced over to Mordacity and let out a relieved sigh. "Least you didn't kill an innocent woman."

"Not from lack of effort." Mordacity rubbed at her neck.

"Told you I was sorry."

She glared at Nero. "Sorry doesn't make my neck stop hurting."

Jayne was aghast. "He really choked you?"

"With his powers, yes."

Hauk held his hands up. "I didn't even have a clue about how to stop it. I was afraid if I shot him, it'd kill her."

Nero gave him a peeved glare. "I wasn't trying to kill her as much as gain information."

Hadrian crossed his arms over his chest. "Did you?"

Nero didn't answer. Cocking his head, he stepped closer to Jayne. "Why can't I hear you?"

"Because I'm being silent."

Nero gave her a droll stare over her sarcasm.

"I can't hear her thoughts either."

His jaw dropped. "Part Trisani?"

"Andarion." Jayne wagged her eyebrows at him.

Hadrian laughed. "She's messing with you. She has some Tris blood."

Nero winced. "She's a *Clusan*?"

Hadrian nodded. Clusas were a very special breed of Trisani. A rare race that should have died out with all the rest of them.

That only seemed to agitate his brother. "You ready to leave?"

"I'm not five."

"No, but you are hunted. I have a place that's safe and clean."

Clean was a nice change of pace. Still, Hadrian shook his head. "I'm not going. I'm done hiding."

"Don't make me stun you and haul you out of here. You know I'm not leaving you while you're being hunted, and you're too minsid heavy to carry. I swear if you make me do that, I'm banging your head into everything I pass."

Hadrian gestured at Nero as he spoke to Jayne. "You still think your sister's the bigger asshole?"

"Reevaluating."

Jayne watched Hadrian. He was so different around Nero. Instead of that air of calm aloofness, he was more like a rabid lorina. "Guess you do lose your composure."

Hadrian jerked his chin toward Nero. "Only around *him*."

"I get it. Only family can make someone who could remain so calm while being shot at lose their shit over nothing."

Hadrian gave her a droll stare. "That why you lost it in the transport?"

Jayne rubbed at her brow. "If you ever meet my sister, you'll completely understand."

"Hang around my brother, and you'll understand my change in tone, too."

Her gaze went to Nero's holster and the emblem it held. "You're guild. Pedarian."

He skimmed her gear and arched his brow. "You're not."

Mordacity answered for her. "She's an Incee. Not an Inca." Incas were contract hitters who worked illegally. Incees were the independents who had no allegiance to any virgyl guild or nation. While they didn't have any backup, they also didn't have any of the hassles that went along with virgyl memberships. Each one came with its own set of rules and problems.

Problems and obligations Eve profaned and refused to be a part of.

Pedarians were one of the largest and more civilized assassin virgyls. They were highly regulated which meant Hadrian's brother wasn't an animal and had rules he had to follow, or they'd punish him.

Jayne relaxed a little at the good news. All the Pedarians she'd ever met had been decent for the most part. While Nero's clansmen might bend the rules a bit to bring in their targets, they were better than most of their ilk.

"So what are we doing, kids?" Hauk leaned against the wall.

"I vote all of you get out of my home."

Jayne shook her head at Mordacity. "I get it."

"Now get out."

Nero tsked at her. "Really?"

Mordacity crossed her arms over her chest. "I told all of you that I have no idea who set me up."

"But I do."

Nero jerked at the sound of another male voice intruding from the darkest corner of the room. "What the hell?"

Jayne didn't react as she saw her brother-in-law step forward.

Jinx sized their group up with a warning look that told them, Trisani or not, Jinx was at the top of this food chain.

His long white-blond hair was pulled back into a braid that fell to the middle of his back. His leather League uniform fit his muscled physique to perfection and announced to any and all onlookers that he was the best of their assassin core.

Which was how he'd no doubt found them in spite of the Tavali shielding.

Standing taller than Nero but just a tad shorter than Hadrian, he was an impressive sight. "You okay, Jaynie?"

"Fine."

"Good." He lifted his dark sunglasses up to rest on top of his head, which took a degree of the lethal aura away from him.

But not much.

Jinx inclined his head to Hadrian's brother. "Nero Scalera. At last we meet."

"I don't know you."

"You don't have to. You have a League file so thick, it reads like an Andarion history text." He paused for a second.

"Should I be nervous?" Mordacity asked.

Jinx smirked. "Jaded. Nice."

Nero turned his scowl toward Jayne. "What's he babbling on about?"

She shrugged. "He often has voices in his head like a

Trisani. Only these are delusional. You kind of get used to it."

Jinx passed an irritated smirk at Jayne. "Your mistake, Scalera, was that the other felon you escaped prison with was captured. Tortured. Gutted. He gave up everything he had on you and Syn. All that info Syn had purged for you was returned to the League database." He tapped his wrist, and a deep voice filled the room.

"Nero Ashter Gordian Scalera. Eldest surviving son of Gisella Verona Scalera and Gaius Ashterius Valeran Scalera both deceased on 8522.23.12 on–"

"Enough." Nero flinched. "I get it. I should have had Syn keep an eye on my files."

Inclining his head, Jinx cut the transmission. "So, the League is now aware both you and little brother survived the holocaust."

Which meant anyone could find out Hadrian was alive.

Ouch.

Jayne crossed her arms over her chest. "So, who did this?"

Jinx shrugged. "Don't know. Don't care. My one and only is getting you back to Eve, safe and sound. They are big grown men and are on their own."

Nero screwed his face up. "Really?"

Jinx straightened up. "Meaning?"

"She came after my brother. I think you're overlooking the law that ties their lives together now."

"I think you're overlooking the fact that I *am* the law."

Nero bristled. "Yeah? Then how do you plan to disentangle them?"

Faster than anyone could blink, Jinx had his blaster drawn and aimed at Hadrian's head. "I kill your brother."

Chapter Seven

Nero flung his hand up as if he were using his powers to disarm Jinx.

Jinx scoffed. "Wasting your time, dumbass. Your powers have no effect on me." He let his blaster fall back in his grip. "Relax. No need in either one of you getting a migraine. I'm not really going to shoot my cousin in the head. No matter how stupid the two of you are."

"Wait . . . what?" Hadrian's jaw fell slack.

"Jinx Teivel. My grandmother was Mazel Scalera."

Now it was Nero's turn to gape. "Amita Mazie?"

He nodded and passed an amused grin at Hadrian. "Your father, Ashter, was my avunculus."

Nero gaped at the disclosure. "I thought all of you were dead."

"Apparently, we're cockroaches. It tends to run in the family."

Jayne shook her head. "I'm so confused."

"Yeah. Politics." Jinx holstered his blaster. "Confuses everybody. Like you and Eve, when you have any Trisani blood, you don't go around letting anyone know it."

"Are we related to her, too?"

Jayne's stomach cramped at Nero's question. *Please tell me I didn't kiss my cousin.*

Jinx visibly cringed. "No. Jayne and Eve are Panteras."

Nero cocked his head. "So, they *are* noble."

"For all the good it never did any of us." Jinx stepped back. "Except to ruin our lives and make us hunted."

He had a point.

"But to answer your question, their branch of the Panteras fell out of favor with your royal house a full generation before the collapse of your empire . . . which is how they managed to survive the purge of your species."

Jayne winced at a truth that still burned. Jinx's branch had survived when his grandmother had married into the royal house of a different empire.

Sadly, Jinx's line had ended when his uncle had killed his father and mother, then sold Jinx into slavery to the League. Now, his uncle ruled while Jinx had no hope of ever being free. Once the League owned an assassin, the only way out was death.

Hadrian frowned at Jinx. "So, if you're not going to really kill me. How do you get Jayne out of this?"

"I'm still going to kill you. Just on paper. Much more permanently than what Syn did earlier."

"He's right," Nero agreed. "If you're alive, she's hunted."

"Exactly." Jinx started typing on his arm. "So, she's going to surrender you to a League agent . . . me. You're going to be executed and then we're going to hide you where the sun doesn't shine."

Hadrian shook his head. "I don't like where the sun doesn't shine."

"Too bad. You're too big, pardon the pun, a risk for us. Nero blends, but you . . ."

"I keep telling him that," Nero said.

It was true. Nero could pass for any human race. But Hadrian held features that clearly marked him as Trisani if anyone were paying attention.

Jayne felt Hadrian's pain, especially after what he'd told her about wanting his freedom. "Can't you hide him with mix-bloods?" She swept her gaze over him. "He's tall enough to pass for Andarion or Hyshian." Those would also explain away his unusual eye color.

Jinx scoffed. "They'd treat him like shit. Andarions are extremely hostile to anything or anyone who isn't one-hundred-percent pure blooded Andarion. You know this. Hyshians are hostile to males of any species. They wouldn't even allow him to speak in public. If you hate him that much, I might as well shoot him in the head. It'd be kinder."

"Personally, I vote for the option of not being shot in the head."

Jinx smirked. "Well, Lord Picky, you're just going to have to settle with whatever options I can come up with."

Nero cleared his throat. "Remember, we're family."

Jinx stared blankly at Nero. "Too soon. Especially given the fact that one half of my family annihilated the other half. I'm only a quarter Tris. The rest of me is bloodthirsty asshole."

"Noted."

Hauk shook his head. "What are you holding back on us, Jinx?"

"Pardon?"

"I might not be Tris, but I can read body language. What's in your head?"

Jinx narrowed his gaze on Mordacity. "You want to elaborate, Nisa?"

She paled at the mention of that name.

"Nisa?" Nero appeared as baffled as Jayne felt.

Mordacity stiffened. "How do you know that name?"

"I'm League. There's nothing I can't find out about anyone. Challenge me."

Mordacity shook her head. "No one should have been able to find my real name."

"Why is that?" Jinx asked.

"Because it was changed by a League member."

Jinx clicked his tongue. "And that's the right answer."

Nero scowled. "Who?"

Mordacity shook her head. "Can't tell you. He'll kill me if I do."

"Pretty sure he's already trying to kill you. Why else would we have this elaborate plot to cause your demise?" Jinx cut his gaze to Nero. "And I'm pretty sure the Scaleras already have that name."

"You can't tell anyone who I'm thinking of." She shook her head again. "He would just kill me if he wanted me dead. Why do something so elaborate?"

"Because you're Tavali." Jayne stepped forward as she understood. "He kills you and they're under oath to retaliate."

Jinx inclined his head to her. "That's one answer . . . Want to finish the tale?" he asked Mordacity.

Mordacity vigorously shook her head this time. "No. It wouldn't happen."

Jinx tsked. "Kyr Zemin has no soul. Why wouldn't he order your death?"

"I know for a fact that he wouldn't. Besides, why frame this to take out two people he doesn't even know? He'd have no interest in Nero or Hadrian. Think bigger."

"What do you mean?"

"Who's the one person who could benefit from all our deaths?"

By the look on Jinx's face, it was obvious that he had no clue.

Neither did Jayne. "Who?"

"We're all three supposed to be dead. The Scaleras were meant to die when their planet fell. I was supposed to be dead when the Phrixian Naglfari leader took out a hit on me. Who would benefit if the three of us were suddenly gone?"

Jinx let out a sound of supreme disgust. "Huwin Quiakides."

She nodded. "The fact that I'm still here after that warrant is a slap in his face."

Nero cursed. "And our territories were used to bribe the League so that he'd be elected Prime Commander."

Jayne scowled at that. "I thought the only way to be a Prime Commander was to assassinate the current one."

Jinx snorted. "No. When the PC dies, there's an election held by our highest-ranking members. They *can* be bribed."

"Yeah, and one of those bastards currently sits on my father's throne." Nero clenched his teeth. "Sorry I doubted you, Mordacity."

"I understand and I don't blame you. It's hard to see the truth when your family's being threatened."

"So what do we do?" Jayne was frustrated at this point.

"Again, we have to kill off your target. There's no other choice." Jinx turned his attention to Mordacity. "As for you . . ."

"I know. I'll have to change my name again."

"You need to vanish. Go so deep underground that Commander Quiakides can't find you."

Suddenly, the door opened.

Everyone in the room, except Mordacity pulled their weapons and aimed them.

Only the person who came through the door was far shorter than where they aimed.

"Mama?" The little girl froze as she saw them and felt the tenseness of their bodies.

"It's okay, Mimi. Come here." Mordacity held her hand out for her daughter.

Jayne was stunned as she holstered her weapon. "How do you hide with a kid?"

"I'll find a way. I always do." She picked the child, who couldn't be any more than four or five, up in her arms and held her close.

Hadrian put his blaster in his pocket, then turned to Jinx. "Am I dead yet?"

"You are. Officially this time. Poor Syn will be devastated that I undid his work."

"Then we need to go." Nero grabbed Hadrian by his sleeve.

But Hadrian shrugged his tight grip away. He moved closer to Jayne. "Thank you for not putting a blast through my skull."

"You're very welcome. Try to stay off my bounty sheets."

"Make no promises." He smiled. "You try not to get suckered by another contract."

A wicked gleam appeared in her eyes. "Make no promises."

Then, he took her hand into his and lifted it to his lips.

Her heart fluttered at the gesture. It was so simple and yet it did the strangest things to her stomach.

In that moment, she didn't want to let him go. But

that was stupid. They were basically strangers. She didn't really know him at all.

He knew even less about her.

Passing strangers.

Yet as he turned and followed after his brother, a part of her ached. It felt as if she were losing part of her heart.

How stupid am I?

Eve would say infinitely.

Damn, she hadn't hurt like this in a long time.

"Ready to go home?"

She blinked at Jinx's question. The answer should be yes and yet . . .

I have no home.

Just a roof over her head and a place to take her meals. Sadly, she couldn't remember ever having a real home.

"Sure."

Hauk stepped back so that she could leave first.

Jayne stopped beside Mordacity. "Thank you for the hospitality." With a smile, she ruffled the girl's hair. "You stay out of trouble."

The little green cutie pulled her thumb out of her mouth. "Okies."

"She's the spitting image of you."

Mordacity smiled. "I know. But I see some of her father in her, too."

By the way she said it, it was obvious that Mordacity had loved the girl's father.

A lot.

Jayne smiled at her. "You two take care."

"You, too."

And with that, Jayne made her way to the hallway. Honestly, she was hoping to catch sight of Hadrian as she left.

He was nowhere to be found.

And that hit her so hard that she actually felt punched. It didn't make sense.

Yet there was no denying how she felt.

Have a nice life, Hadrian. She meant it. Someone deserved to have their dream. If it couldn't be her, she wanted him to have his.

* * *

Hadrian paused as they reached Nero's fighter. He'd kept looking back, wanting Jayne to be there.

She wasn't.

Why should she be?

Really. What could he offer her? Everything he owned was in the backpack he hated.

One that seemed to get heavier as he climbed Nero's fighter ladder and settled himself into the backseat.

Memories of Jayne haunted him.

Nero climbed up. But instead of taking his seat, he sat on the side and stared at Hadrian. "What are you doing?"

"Waiting on you to take me to whatever backwater hell hole you can find."

"What about your ship?"

"What about it?"

Nero arched a brow. "You're actually leaving it?"

"Why not? I've no attachment to it. If I use it, you have a stroke." He adjusted his backpack in his lap. "I'm through fighting you. I'm just going to go with the flow. Dump me wherever."

"Well, that would have been nice a few years ago. Now . . ."

"Now what?"

"You heard what Jinx said. You're free. Or dead. But

basically the same thing. You don't have to hide anymore. You can use your fake ID, or have Syn create a new one for you, and you can live wherever you want."

Hadrian didn't know what to say to that. All this time, he'd lived under Nero's shadow. The thought of being able to step out into the daylight . . .

He had no reaction for it.

"Seriously?"

Nero swept his arm around the bay. "The universe awaits. Just please keep in touch. 'Cause if I have to hunt you down, I will kick your gargantuan ass."

Hadrian snorted. "All right." He got up and started down the ladder.

Sadness haunted Nero's eyes. That expression wrung a deep ache inside him.

"I'll keep in touch." He pulled his brother in for a tight hug.

Nero clapped him on the back. "You better." He released him.

Hadrian took a second before he left and headed across the bay to where his own ship was docked.

Freedom. It'd been the only thing he'd ever wanted. To make his own decisions and not hide himself.

Now that he had it, he wasn't sure what to do with it. He'd lived so many places . . .

Outposts. Planets. Stations. Hell, he'd even camped on an asteroid once.

No matter where he'd been, he'd always been lonely. Afraid to make friends.

He could do that now.

Stunned with disbelief, he got into his ship and fired the engines.

"Here I come universe . . . Get out of my way."

Chapter Eight

SIX MONTHS LATER

J ayne sighed as she saw the credits hit her account. It hadn't been a big bounty, but no one had died.

And she hadn't bled.

Yet she wasn't as happy as she should be, and she knew it. No matter how much she tried, she just couldn't forget Hadrian. Every assignment she took reminded her of the incredible man she'd known for just a brief time.

I've got to get over this.

Her door buzzed.

She wasn't really paying attention as she opened it, thinking it was Eve who was due for a lunch date.

So, when it slid open to show her a very tall, gorgeous Tris, all she could do was stand there, gaping.

Hadrian screwed his face up. "Still, can't read you. Are you happy see me, or pissed?"

Without thinking, she launched herself at him with such force that it knocked him back.

Wrapping his arms around her and laughing, he held her close as she kissed him with everything she had.

"I'm going to take it that you're happy."

More than she could even explain. "What are you doing here?"

He handed her is ID. "I took your advice and bought a condo not far away."

Confused, she looked at it and saw his alias. It also listed him as a Hyshian male.

"Isn't it illegal for a male to live alone?"

"Technically, yes. But I was hoping that I might be able to persuade this incredible woman I know to have some mercy on me. Keep me out of jail."

Those words made her heart sing. Yet she was terrified to let herself jump to any conclusion. "What kind of proposition is this?"

He shrugged. "The best I could come up with on short notice. I never was one much for creativity."

Jayne shut her door and stared at him. He was thinner than he'd been, and his hair was longer.

Still, he was absolutely stunning.

But that didn't stop her from being a little pissed off about this. "You vanish for six months with no contact whatsoever and you think, what? You can just come back and pick me up?"

At least he had the decency to look sheepish. "Not exactly. Jinx told me to stay away until he was sure no one was coming back for me. You can call him and ask. I didn't want to endanger you." He reached into his backpack and pulled out an envelope. "And I come bearing gifts."

Really, he was the best gift she could have hoped for. She couldn't imagine anything better.

Until she pulled the documents out of his folder. Disbelief, shock, happiness, and incredulity warred as she tried to make sense of what he'd given her. "Is this for real?"

Smiling, he nodded. "Syn pulled strings with his school. You've been accepted into their teaching program."

Tears welled in her eyes.

"Why would you do this?"

Pain darkened his eyes. "I can't get you out of my mind, Jayne. I've been absolutely miserable without you."

"But you've made yourself a Hyshian. Do you understand what that means?"

A slow smile spread over his face. "Freedom alone is worthless. I know it's been brief, but no one brings me the peace and happiness that you do. I want your face to be the first one I see in the morning and the last one I see at night."

A single tear fled down her cheek. "I love you, Hadrian."

"And I love you, Jayne. I always will."

Epilogue

FIFTEEN YEARS LATER

Jayne smiled as Hadrian handed her their their most recent addition to their family.

Sway Jinx Erixour.

He was the most handsome baby she'd ever seen. "He looks like you."

Hadrian wrinkled his nose. "You're delirious from your delivery. He looks like a squashed elf."

"Don't you listen to daddy, my angel. He's just jealous there's another man in my life."

He laughed. "Not even a little. I don't need my powers to know I will always rank second to this one."

Her hospital door opened to allow their two daughters to spill into the room. They were closely followed by her sister and Jinx.

"Can I see?"

"Can I hold him?"

As always, her girls talked over each other as they scrambled onto her bed and shoved their father out of the way. Hadrian's expression said that he didn't mind in the least.

Eve shook her head as she and Jinx watched them.

"I want a baby!" Tara, their oldest, shouted over her younger sister, Lyra.

Hadrian squelched his laughter. "I'm standing down on this one, Ma. You're the one who has to explain those mechanics to her. I'm not about to."

"We'll talk about this in a few more years, baby. Eight is way too young to be a mom. For now, you can practice on your little brother."

She rolled her eyes and sighed. "Okay. If I must."

Jayne carefully placed Sway in his sister's arms. She ran her hand through Tara's curls as love washed over her.

So much had changed over the last fifteen years. She'd been a teacher and had gone back to contract work to keep her family safe.

But more than that, to help Nykyrian, Syn, Hauk, Jinx, Nero, Eve and so many others reshape the corrupt League that had preyed on all of them.

They were still fighting the authorities, but she liked to think that in a small way, she'd played a part in making the universe a better place.

The only thing she knew for certain was that Hadrian had made her small world worth living.

"You okay?"

She took Hadrian's hand and smiled at him. "I am. Just thinking how grateful I am that you can read our children's thoughts."

Laughing, he kissed her and then Tara's head. "Especially this one. She's got too much of her mother in her."

Jinx picked up Lyra who squealed in delight.

Jayne didn't miss the sadness in her sister's eyes. Because the League still owned Jinx, they didn't dare have children of their own.

Her heart ached for her sister. All they could do was pray that the rebellion Jayne and her friends had started would free him the way he'd freed her and Hadrian.

"Congrats." Eve kissed her on her cheek, then kissed Sway. By the way her sister's eyes shined, she knew Eve meant it. There was no jealousy or hard feelings.

It was why she loved her, too.

"To new beginnings." Jayne squeezed her hand.

Eve smiled as she held her hand out to Hadrian and he took it. "And to family."

After all, family was forever. They were united by mutual respect. Sacrifice.

But most of all, they were united by love.

Forever and always.

MyKENYON
READ IT. LOVE IT
www.sherrilynkenyon.com

Defying all odds is what #1 New York Times and international bestselling author Sherrilyn Kenyon does best. Rising from extreme poverty as a child that culminated in being a homeless mother with an infant, she has become one of the most popular and influential authors in the world (in both adult and young adult fiction), with dedicated legions of fans known as Paladins–thousands of whom proudly sport tattoos from her numerous genre-defying series.

Since her first book debuted in 1993 while she was still in college, she has placed more than 80 novels on the New York Times list in all formats and genres, including manga and graphic novels, and has more than 70 million books in print worldwide. Her current series include: Dark-Hunters®, Chronicles of Nick®, Deadman's Cross™, Black Hat Society™, Nevermore™, Silent Swans™, Lords of Avalon® and The League®.

Over the years, her Lords of Avalon® novels have been adapted by Marvel, and her Dark-Hunters® and Chronicles of Nick® are New York Times bestselling manga and comics and are #1 bestselling adult coloring books.

Join her and her Paladins online at QueenofAll-
Shadows.com and www.facebook.com/mysherrilyn.

Milton Keynes UK
Ingram Content Group UK Ltd.
UKHW042014020224
437187UK00004B/130

9 781648 392832